International Best Selling Author

KateMarie Collins

Amari:

Three Tales of
Love and Triumph

Solstice Publishing - www.solsticepublishing.com

To Lindsey —
Enjoy!

Amari:

Three Tales

Of

Love and Triumph

By

KateMarie Collins

1/19/2020

KateMarie Collins

Book One:
Fin's Magic

Dedication

For my grandparents

J. Carroll and Myra M. Duff

Who taught me what it meant to love another person in this

life. And the next.

Chapter One

*T*hunk.

The sound of the arrow piercing the wild boar's carcass seemed loud in the early morning silence. Fin lowered her bow. "Well, at least I hit it that time."

"Your aim's getting better. It may not convince a trained archer, but most won't question your role with us. That should make things easier for you." Alaric kept his voice low.

She reached over her shoulder and extracted another arrow from her quiver. Nocking it into place, she slowly drew back the string. "Easy hasn't been part of my vocabulary for a very long time." She let the string go, wincing as the string bit into her arm. "And fooling most of the people isn't good enough." Fin rubbed at her stinging skin as she watched the arrow fly. It landed in the ground at least a yard away from the boar.

"Come on, let's go pick them up and try again." Alaric motioned for her to follow him.

They kept their voices low as they passed the small tents where their companions slept. No sense in waking them up before dawn, not unless something showed up. The last few days had been tough on all of them. After the way they'd left Lorien, Fin still kept her ears open. She didn't like the feeling of being chased. But it was better than being chained.

"Fin, relax. If anyone made out what you are in town, they'd have caught up to us by now."

She shook her head, the red braid dancing down her back. "You know I can't. The only reason I'm still free is because I don't relax. If I relax, this happens." She looked at him.

Fin watched as Alaric's face turned momentarily to amazement as she flashed the true color of her eyes at him. The normal green was gone, replaced by the metallic gold that marked her as one of the Amari. She sighed.

"It's beautiful, you know. They're beautiful. It's a shame you have to hide them. Even around us." Alaric's voice was barely above a whisper.

"Yeah, well, hiding them has kept me out of chains for twenty years. It's a habit now." Fin bent down and picked up her arrow. "I read somewhere once there used to be thousands of us. Walking the streets, not hiding. I haven't met another Amari for over ten years, not one who didn't belong to someone." A wistful tone crept into her voice.

Alaric's hand on her shoulder made her look up. "You don't have to hide around me. No one should be treated like that, ever. And I won't let that happen to you."

The look he gave her sent chills down her spine. Of all her companions, he was the one she talked to the most. Put all her trust in. Emile, Trystian, and Gwen were all there to protect her, hide her, and she knew it. But there was something about Alaric that told her his interest went even farther.

His focus changed to something behind her. She made sure her eyes were hidden again. That was the first bit of magic she learned how to do. It was the only thing that had kept her free for so long.

"In the camp!" A male voice called out from the surrounding brush. "We're cold tonight. Can we share your fire?"

Fin hurriedly gathered the last of her arrows, then darted back to wake the others. Alaric's voice carried across the small area. "Depends. Are you friend or foe? We don't take kindly to those who would share our fire and try to rob us blind."

Fin rushed into the first tent, shaking Gwen awake. A single finger to her lips was all the warning the dark haired woman needed. Slipping back out, Fin could see three men emerging from the forest not far from Alaric's tall form. No armor, no uniform, but something wasn't right about how they walked.

"Would we ask first if we were foes? Why not just rob you? Why give your pet time to warn the others?" Fin stiffened at the word the man used to describe her. *Pet*. That's what a chained Amari was called. She dove into the second tent. Emile caught her within his embrace. "Shh. There's no guarantee they know."

Trystian was up as well, strapping his sword belt on. "Stay close. We'll keep you safe." The tall, bearded man reassured her before leading the way out of the tent.

"What pet? There's none here. If that's what you seek, you're in the wrong place." Alaric's voice was even. It was always better to talk their way out of a conflict.

The first tendrils of light from the approaching dawn gave her enough to see what she feared. All three of the men approaching Alaric had chains dangling from their belts.

"Ah, that's fine. Charlie here--" the leader jerked his head back towards one of his companions, "--he likes to pretend he can smell 'em. Says they smell bad on account of being corrupted by that magic of theirs." He kicked at the dead boar Fin and Alaric had used for target practice. "Seems to me this is what he was smelling."

"Fire's that way." Alaric gestured towards the rest of them. Fin tried not to grip her bow too tightly. The others stood near enough to prevent anyone from reaching her, but far enough away to pull out their weapons if it became necessary.

"Much obliged," the leader remarked as he motioned the others to follow. Fin watched the strangers approach, Alaric trailing close behind. Something wasn't right about them. It went beyond the shackles.

Alaric raised his chin, calling out "We have guests."

That's when it happened.

The lead bounty hunter threw his fist back hard, knocking Alaric to the ground. Fin fumbled with her quiver, sending out the silent healing energy to her friend. Around her, the other three drew their weapons and prepared to meet the charging foes.

By the time she got an arrow nocked, they were too close. Fin retreated a few feet, watching the fighting closely. Her bow was ready, but she needed to get a clear shot.

Close combat always unnerved her. The stench of blood turned her stomach. Gwen was holding her own against the one named Charlie, and winning handily. When the first body dropped, Fin relaxed just a little. There weren't many out there who could beat Trystian or Emile in one-on-one combat, because the two men didn't believe in mercy. Just an expedient death.

An arrow buzzed past her ear, the fletching scratching her cheek. Spinning on her heels, she watched it sail past the man charging at her. He leaped to tackle her as she tried to raise her bow. Instinct kicked in, and she did the only thing she could think of to stop him.

She willed his heart to stop beating.

An anguished wail tore from her throat. Pain forced her to her knees and caused her to drop her bow. The body of her would-be assailant fell with a heavy thud in front of her. Fin grasped at her left arm, desperate to breathe through the searing agony rippling down her bicep. She'd killed him. Justified or not, she'd taken a life.

"Fin? Are you okay?" Alaric's voice broke through the shock. She opened her eyes.

He knelt in front of her. A single hand gently brushed her hair from her face. Concern for her was clearly visible in his brown eyes.

"I…I killed him." She could barely whisper the words.

Chapter Two

Captain Roberts watched the fight unfold. The fools. That had to be the dumbest set of bounty hunters he'd ever seen. The one remaining hidden was fairly good, but still clumsy. No wonder it'd taken them three days to catch up with the Amari and her friends.

When she killed the one, he knew it was time to move. He signaled to one of the men behind him. "Get everyone mounted, move around to surround them. But don't come out until my signal." He turned to the man to his right. "James, come with me. I might need your help convincing her to come quietly. We'll go in on foot." He nodded once, assured that his men would do as he ordered without hesitation. They always did.

Roberts looked back towards the makeshift campsite. Three of them were moving to pack up gear. The Amari still remained on the ground, the archer comforting her. She favored her left arm.

"The scar will be deep for that," James remarked in a low voice. "The physical pain will not cease for days."

"What about the rest of it?" Roberts asked.

James turned to face him. The metallic gaze of his always amazed Roberts. No matter how often he'd seen it. "The mark on her soul will remain. We do not forget any death we cause, no matter how justified."

He nodded in understanding. "Keep your eyes hidden for now. When we need them to know what you are, we'll reveal it." With that, he stepped out of the edge of the woods and into the dawn-drenched clearing.

He didn't announce himself. He just walked. They would see him, or he and James would stop close enough they didn't have to scream and alert anyone else lurking in the woods.

The other woman saw them first. She slapped the arm of the two helping her pack up camp. Swords came out quickly. They were well trained. Roberts could appreciate that. All three moved to take positions to defend the Amari. The archer was helping her to stand. He and James were close enough now to see her face clearly. Pain marred the pale skin. She was not well.

"That's close enough, soldier." The bearded man spoke, his accent giving away his identity. That helped Roberts immensely. He had names, but not descriptions, of the Amari's companions. "We do not need assistance from you. The corpses are those of some ruffians who set on us. We just defended ourselves. Go keep the King's Peace elsewhere."

Roberts spread his hands wide, keeping his sword in its sheath. "Have no worries, Trystian. We saw the fight and know who started it. We're not here to arrest you, just deliver an invitation."

Suspicion crossed the faces of the ones he could see. "I don't blame you for your caution. There are many out there who would send better men than the ones you dispatched in hopes to find your companion. And chain her. My liege is not one of those. He would help her, offer her sanctuary." He walked a few more steps, staying just out of sword range. "Not all feel the Amari are dangerous unless leashed. I can show you the proof of that." He looked at James and nodded.

The reaction was what he hoped for. The one he thought was Emile glanced back and whispered something to the archer. Roberts still wasn't certain he had the names right between those two.

"What is it you want from us? We only wish to be left alone, travel in peace." The archer spoke, cinching his identity. Alaric, the Islander.

"We only offer sanctuary while you're in my King's lands. We will not prevent you from leaving. He knew you roamed near and would take counsel with you. Give you the chance to rest, recover. Meet more of your kind."

"How do you know what I am?" The voice of the woman rose up from behind the group. They parted, giving Roberts the first real look at her. Her shirt was ripped and bloodstained, her red hair escaping from a single braid and framing her tired, pained face. She did not hide her eyes from him.

James dropped to his knee in front of Roberts. "We know because we would not give up hope, Your Highness. Please, let us help you. Trust is not easy among us, but I would give my life up willingly if we deceive you in this. King Christoph is friend of the Amari, not foe. Let me prove it to you."

Roberts was taken aback. James had told him nothing of her being royal. From the looks of her companions, they were as stunned as he was.

"And if we refuse?"

Roberts raised his arm, waving his fingers once. The rest of his men, all seventy-five, slowly emerged from the forest. Ringing them with a mounted force. "I'm really sorry, but I'm going to have to insist. His Majesty is most anxious to talk with you."

* * * *

He didn't try to engage them in conversation. They took only two horses. Alaric rode behind the Amari, while Gwen took the other horse. The other two walked, hands on the reins of their companions' horses. The expressions on their faces made it obvious that they didn't trust him, especially after he called out his troops. Roberts sighed. He really didn't want to do that, but the King had been adamant. Find them, find *her*, and bring her back to the safety of the castle. Lorien was at the very border of the kingdoms, and tensions were high between the countries. Roberts had pushed his men hard to try and get here before King Lor sent out his own troops to find her. Another league, though, and they'd be far enough into Caerlynn where he could relax. Even Lor wouldn't cross the border that far.

"Except that we did, Captain, and he could see that as a violation of the treaty." James' voice was low.

"Treaty or not, we had orders. Though a little more information from you would've been nice! What possessed you to not mention she was the last member of the Royal Family?"

James shrugged, "I wasn't sure she was, not until I saw her. From the look on her face, she has no idea herself. The story has been told so many times, you wonder how much is true and how much has been added by a bard."

"I want to hear this story, sir. I don't know it." Fin's voice sounded from behind them. Roberts turned in his saddle, glancing back at her. Her voice wasn't as unsteady as before. The pain was still marring her features, but it was less pronounced than it had been when they first mounted up. She wore more of a mask now, of her own creating. He nodded to James, the two moving far enough apart to give her horse space to join them.

"It doesn't surprise me, Your Highness, that you--" Raising her right hand, Fin cut him off.

"Don't call me that. It's not my title to claim, nor yours to bestow. I want the story, not the truth as you see it."

James nodded. "As you wish. Twenty-two years ago, the Amari still had a home, and a ruler. It wasn't much of one. It was more a series of caves in the Eastern Mountains. But we did what we could to remain undetected. When we could, we'd try to free any of our kind who had been chained. That was our ultimate downfall." He paused. "A group went to rescue one such slave. And they did. But she betrayed us all. She told her master how to find us. When the bounty hunters came, she even used her magic against those of us who fought. In the end, everyone who had lived free under the mountain was dead or in chains. Everyone but one small girl."

He looked right at Fin. "The youngest daughter of the King, Serafina by name, was scooped up by her nurse and she carried the toddler to the underground river. She placed the girl into a small basket and used her own magic to propel the craft quickly downriver. When the hunters found the woman, she claimed she drowned the child rather than hand her over to a life of servitude. There are some who believe that, one day, the child will return and lead us to freedom."

Roberts swore to himself. From the tone of James' voice, he believed every word of the story. Christoph was a just King, unlike his father. Sheltering the Amari was one thing. Helping with an open rebellion? That wasn't something Roberts thought he'd be able to stomach.

"Interesting story, but that doesn't tell me why you think I'm this lost child. The name's common. I doubt I'm the only one within the Amari whose ever been saddled with it." There was an edge to her voice that alarmed Robert. Casually, he listened closely to the exchange between her and James.

The look on James' face changed as he looked at her. Was that adoration? Infatuation? Idolatry? Damn! He'd talk with the man later, when they stopped for the night. The last thing he needed was for him to get besotted by a pretty face that might be royalty.

"A few things. The child had red hair, the only one in the royal family for the last three generations. It's common enough among humans, yes. But among the Amari the trait is very recessive and hardly comes to pass. Your age is right. She would be twenty-five now, and you are close to the same age." He hesitated.

'Don't stop now. You're spinning quite a tale." Alaric spoke up. Roberts glanced at the Islander who sat behind Fin on the horse. His face had hardened, his posture more guarded. The arm encircling her waist tightened. James was treading on thin ice with the man. The intelligence he'd been given didn't mention any romantic leanings, but it hadn't talked about her being potential royalty either.

James turned his attention to Alaric. "We Amari can sense things. Things that humans cannot. We know when someone is lying, or if they are destined for greatness. Once she is back with her *own kind*, she will learn how to do this herself." The emphasis on those two words was enough for Roberts. This stopped. Now.

"James!" he snapped. "Ride ahead. The waystation's not far from here. Give them warning of our approach. Arrange for rooms for our guests and have something hot waiting for us to eat."

"One room's all we'll need." Trystian spoke. "We're used to sleeping in rotation. No need for more than the one. We aren't going anywhere."

Rather than argue, Roberts nodded in agreement. One room would be easier for his men to watch than five anyway. At least, he hoped it would be.

Once James had ridden out of earshot, Roberts spoke up again. "I apologize for his behavior, my lady. James is a bit reactionary. Above all, he would see his people have their own lands again. He thinks it would be better for the Amari to live apart from the rest of the world. My king does not agree. He feels we should live peacefully side by side."

"There aren't many who would agree with his views." Fin's voice, though calm, was still guarded.

"That's the truth. His father didn't, that's for certain. Two weeks after he died, though, Christoph personally unchained each Amari his father had collected during his lifetime. He gave them the option of going out into the world or staying there under his protection. Any that stayed would be expected to do a job, but not their magic."

"Magic is banned, then?"

"No. It's more that he doesn't command them to do it. All the jobs they were given required manual labor. Anything from helping around the keep to blacksmithing to farming. A few were asked to join his small council. James was the only one to volunteer to help scout for more Amari, though. He's a good man."

Alaric's head bent nearer to the woman's ear and he whispered something that Roberts couldn't hear. She found it funny, though, as her face brightened slightly and she giggled.

Rather than ask, Roberts turned his focus back to the road ahead. A warm meal was going to do him wonders tonight.

Chapter Three

The waystation wasn't much more than a large house with a barn, but Fin was elated to see it in the distance. Maybe now she'd be able to examine the fresh scar in privacy. Sleep, on a bed no less, also called her. The toll of the day's events had left her bordering on exhaustion. If Alaric's arm hadn't been around her during the long ride here, she would've fallen off her horse.

"We need to talk, the five of us. Alone." Alaric whispered in her ear. She nodded in agreement. Everything had been a blur since she'd killed her assailant. Shock and pain had ruled her thoughts for most of the day. Through it all, Alaric had been right there. He'd whispered to her throughout the ride, reminding her who was talking. Giving her something to grasp while she worked through the events.

She eased her left arm out of the sling Alaric had insisted she wear. She moved her fingers slowly, testing the strength that had returned versus the pain that remained. Grasping her bow was still out of the question, but it was getting better.

"Put it back, Fin. You're surrounded by an army. If we get out of this, it won't be your bow that we'll need." Alaric chided her.

She laughed a little, sliding the arm back into the cloth. "And me playing the invalid will? Maybe I should just play at being a snobby noble. That might get us farther."

"Shh. Later." His lips brushed against her ear. A shiver ran down her spine at the touch. The pain retreated for a moment as her mind wondered what it would be like to feel those lips on hers. "Your admirer is back."

Fin looked over the ears of her horse to see James at the front of four other guardsmen. They waited just outside the gate to the stables.

"Everything's ready." A different shudder ran through her as she felt his gaze fall on her. He wasn't going to give up his idea of her being some long overdue savior easily.

The captain barked out orders to the rest of the troops to set up camp around the waystation. His horse wheeled to face her. "There's a room inside for you and your friends, my lady. And the food is ready if you're hungry. We can leave our horses here and they'll be taken care of."

She waited for Alaric to dismount first, then swung her right leg over the saddle. A pair of strong arms grabbed her waist, lifting her the rest of the way off the horse. After her feet were firmly planted on the ground, she spun around, prepared to thank Alaric for his help. Only it wasn't him that stood behind her. It was James. Alaric stood just off to the side, a scowl on his face. There was something possessive in how James looked at her. One she didn't like at all.

"Come on, then. I'm hungry" Emile shoved himself between her and James, gently grasping the elbow of her left arm and leading her inside.

"I don't trust him, Fin. He wants something from you." Emile's voice, a low whisper, barely reached her ears. "Alaric went to help you down and that guy almost shoved him to the ground to beat him there. I fear what he would do to you." They walked through the single wooden door and into the warm common room.

The huge fireplace dominated the room. A woman bent over a roast turning over the fire, slicing off pieces of meat. A kettle sent out the smells of potatoes, carrots, and spices. The small bar and a few tables with mismatched chairs and benches filled the rest of the space. A single staircase leading upstairs told her where the rooms were.

Gwen pulled out a chair near the fire and forced Fin to sit in it. The table was barely big enough for the five of them, and they made sure they were the only ones who sat there. A younger girl, maybe fifteen, started to set plates of food in front of them. Fin's stomach growled loudly, making her giggle in embarrassment.

"What's so funny?" James spoke from behind her.

All mirth evaporated. She focused on the plate in front of her. "Nothing. It's a private joke"

"Table's full." Trystian announced as everyone else became very intent on eating the food in front of them.

Eventually, he moved away. "Eat, then we go upstairs. I want to get out from under his thumb." Trystian grumbled. "I know he's the same as you, Fin, but his eyes give me the creeps."

"You're not alone," she muttered.

"Where'd he go to, Emile? I can't see without turning my head." Gwen spoke quietly.

Emile raised his head, his dark eyes scanning the room quickly. "He's with the Captain. Looks like he's getting a lecture, but not hearing any of it. He's focused on us."

"Not on us, on me." Fin pushed her plate toward the center. Her appetite vanished. All she wanted was privacy, downtime. It wasn't happening down here.

Trystian shoved his plate away. "I'll handle it. You guys finish up real fast." The large man rose from his chair and moved toward Roberts and James.

"Key, please. We're done and want to get some sleep. It's been a long day." He held out one massive hand.

Fin watched as the Captain looked over at them, then said something in a low voice that she couldn't hear. Trystian made sure his response would carry across the room.

"You said we're not prisoners, just guests. You don't lock guests in their room. Either give me the key, or we're leaving. Now."

A nudge at her elbow broke her concentration. Alaric nodded toward the staircase. Gwen and Emile were already starting to climb the first few steps. She glanced back towards the table where Trystian towered over the two military men. The Captain placed a key in Trystian's outstretched palm. James, though, kept his gaze firmly locked on her. For a moment, Fin understood why so many people reacted like they did to the Amari. The sensation of being the focus of James' stare was chilling. More than anything, she wanted to get someplace where he couldn't watch her. She grasped the plain wood handrail firmly, forcing herself to keep a normal pace up the flight of stairs.

The upper level was without ornamentation. Four doors, each with a number scrawled on it. "It's number three," Trystian muttered as he brushed past her. "Down this way."

The floorboards creaked a little. "Won't have to worry they can sneak up on us. I like it." Emile kept his tone light, randomly stepping from one loose board to another. Fin knew what he was doing. He'd done it every time they dared to stay indoors over the last twenty years. To anyone else, he was being annoying. What he really was doing was determining where they could step without being heard if they had to sneak out. It'd come in handy more than once.

Trystian unlocked their room and pushed the door inward. As anxious as she was to have some sense of privacy, Fin waited in the hallway. Gwen and Trystian would sweep the room, making sure it was safe. *One day*, she thought, *I'll find somewhere I can live and not have to worry about this.*

Gwen's face appeared around the doorframe. "All clear." Fin moved forward, knowing Alaric and Emile would follow.

The room itself was larger than she anticipated. Three beds, with real mattresses and quilts. A pair of bedside tables between them. A small fire had been lit in the fireplace, lending some warmth to the room. Two sturdy wooden chairs sat near the hearth, with their packs in a pile nearby. A screen separated a small alcove from the rest of the room. Peeking behind it, Fin saw a washbasin, pitcher, bar of soap and coarse towel. Not quite a tub, but they'd be able to clean up some.

"Fin, you and Gwen go ahead. We'll sleep in shifts. Emile, you and Gwen take first watch. Wake up me and Alaric in about six hours." Trystian started to unbuckle his sword belt. "Fin, it's none of my business, but you might consider changing your shirt while you're cleaning up."

She looked down at her shirt. The torn garment was spattered with dried blood. She grabbed her pack and yanked out the first shirt she found. It was still dirty, but it didn't have blood on it. Her hands flew to her waist, frantically pulling at the shirt while she sprinted for the screen. It needed to come off. Now. Even if the blood didn't belong to the one she'd killed, her mind recoiled from the sight of it. As soon as she was behind the screen, she removed the offending garment. "Burn it," she commanded, tossing it over the top of the screen. Her hand shook as she tried to pick up the heavy pitcher.

"Fin, put it down. I'll pour the water." Gwen's gentle voice washed over her.

Fin nodded, putting the pitcher back on the table. "Sorry. It's just…just… ." She couldn't describe it.

"I know. It's not an easy thing to do. For your kind it seems even more so." Gwen stood with her back to Fin. Fin waited while the water was poured into the basin.

"There. Here's the soap…oh, Fin." Gwen turned and stopped speaking, her eyes focused on Fin's arm.

Fin swallowed before looking. The deep red scar stretched from her shoulder to her elbow. No wonder she was having trouble grasping things with her hand.

"Everything okay?" Emile called out, concern in his voice.

Fin met Gwen's worried blue eyes. "It's fine," she called out. She took the soap from her friend's hand. "Just a scratch. You've had worse."

Gwen nodded and moved to leave the alcove. "I'll wash up when you're done," she said in a low voice.

Fin stepped closer to the washbasin and tested the water. It wasn't as cold as she feared. Working the bar of soap into a lather, she called out to the rest of the room. "So, what's the plan? Do we sneak out tonight or stay put?" Slowly, she drew a wet corner of the towel over her body, concentrating on getting some of the dirtier sections clean. The scar would wait for the end, if she touched it at all.

"I don't think we can sneak out of here," Emile offered. "There's bound to be guards either sleeping up here, or posted in the hallway. Whoever this King Christoph is, he wants to talk to you. Bad enough to risk open warfare with King Lor. Few send armed troops into that realm without getting just that."

"Roberts seems reasonable. His second, though. James. He wants something from you, Fin. Even if we meet with this king and everything is what Roberts says, that one will cause problems." Trystian said. "I'm of half a mind that we make it seem like you're involved with one of us just to get him to stop staring."

"I'll do it." Alaric's voice sent shivers down Fin's spine. "It would make sense, since I ride with her. A few well-placed threats if he tries to touch her again wouldn't hurt, either. You okay with that, Fin?"

Her heart skipped a beat. Was she okay with it? He was asking permission? Normally, the plans were made and she went along with them. "Um, sure. I think we can make that work." Without thinking, she drew the rough cloth over the new scar. A new wave of pain made her suck in her breath so she didn't scream. Using her right hand only, she somehow got the towel back on its' hook and picked her clean shirt off the floor. The material was softer, but still would irritate the scar. Then again, most things would for a few days yet. At least she didn't have to worry about infection.

She didn't bother tucking it into her breeches. Sleep was what she needed. "So, we play along for now? See what this King wants with me? Alaric and I cozy up to each other and get out of town if things look bad?" Walking out from behind the screen, she maneuvered toward the closest bed.

"Center one's yours, Fin. Don't argue." Trystian glared at her. "We're going to have to be careful. If there's as many of your kind there as we've been told, it might do you some good. Maybe you can learn a few things that'll help you stay hidden."

"And what if all we've heard is true? Would you want to stay?" Emile spoke from a chair near the fire. He raised his head, looking at her carefully. "We all swore to help you, keep you safe. Would you have further need of us?"

Fin sat on her bed. The future Emile mentioned wasn't one she'd ever truly considered. The idea was a dream, nothing more. "You found me hiding in a sewer, Emile. I was what, three? Five? I was convinced the filth would disguise me. Until the hunters tracked me down. If you hadn't been sneaking around down there when it happened, I wouldn't be here. I'd be in some pen, forced to do magic or dead from it." She paused, then looked at the man who'd been so instrumental in her survival. "It wouldn't be much of a thank you for me to turn my back on you at the suggestion of a dream. Until I can walk down a street anywhere we choose to go and not have to hide my eyes, I will need you. Even a sanctuary can be raided."

"Fair enough." He leaned back in the chair, chiding her with a single finger. "I do not sneak. I just move very silently."

Fin joined the others in the laughter that followed. Emile's abilities had kept them out of more trouble than she could count. And made it so Gwen and Trystian didn't have to draw their swords as often.

Crawling under the heavy quilt, she rolled over to her right side. The last thing she saw before she drifted off to sleep was Alaric's face lying on the pillow, one cot over. He was smiling at her.

Chapter Four

"We're almost there. Caerlynn's just around the next bend. Your gear will be taken to your rooms, and I'll take you to meet King Christoph. The first meeting's going to be brief, but I'm sure he'll want to talk with you at length within the next day or two." Roberts informed Fin as she and Alaric rode alongside him.

They'd left the waystation that morning. She'd seen Emile talking to James as they waited for their horses to be saddled. The way he played with one of his daggers at the same time was masterful. What he said, she didn't know. The ruse was started, though, and James had been silent the entire day. His face was a storm cloud every time he'd look at Alaric sitting behind her.

Alaric was playing his part to the hilt. He made sure to pull her closer or kiss the top of her head every time they felt James' gaze on them. She really didn't mind. Each kiss warmed her.

"We'd much prefer to stay together. Captain. I hope you understand. We've been on the road so long together, it would be odd to be alone."

Roberts coughed into his hand. "I do understand, but the decision is not mine. When you speak with my liege privately, you can make that request. Until then, however, you'll have to remain in the rooms assigned to you."

A single rider approached from the front of the column. "Caerlynn's in sight. What message do you want me to give?"

"Tell His Majesty that our mission was successful and we bring five guests with us. Oh, and have the staff notified to get the baths ready. I'm sure they'll want to use them soon after arrival." Roberts snapped off his orders, then watched the messenger ride off. "I mean no offense. After a month on patrol, you learn how nice it is to come home to a hot bath." He gave Fin a crooked smile. "I'm sure I smell more like my horse than my wife likes."

Fin smiled. "A bath is most welcome. Thank you for your consideration."

The road bent, and her eyes went wide. Caerlynn wasn't some small outlying keep. It was a small city. Spreading out across the grassland, the massive stone walls warned everyone who would lay siege to the town that it wasn't going to fall without a struggle. Archers walked the parapet, pointing to the troops coming home.

As she passed through the thick wood and iron gate, she craned her neck, trying hard to take in all the sights and sounds around her. Children screamed for joy about their father returning, women stood in the doorways of the surrounding homes. The neatly-lined streets led further into the town. It was slow going, but that was fine with her. On every corner, mixed in with the cheering crowds, was an Amari. Smiling, waving, shouting greetings. Not hiding, and not in chains.

At last they got to the stables. As they waited their turn, Fin saw one of the soldiers run toward an Amari woman. There was joy on her face at seeing him. He stopped in front of her and held his hands palms up.

"If you call," he said.

"You will come," the woman answered, placing her hands in his before embracing him.

"Captain, what was that about?" Fin asked, curious.

He'd dismounted and was holding the reins of her horse while Alaric slid off. Her waist warmed at the touch of Alaric's hands around her as he helped her down. "It's an Amari custom. Wallace isn't Amari, but his wife is. There's some kind of connection between mates and the ritual is part of it. If one is leaving, the other will 'listen' for their call if there is trouble. And try to find them if it comes. When they return, the ritual is reversed because the one who stayed behind has called them home." He shrugged. "I don't really understand it, but I've seen it happen. Come, King Christoph is anxious to greet you properly to his home."

Fin tore her gaze from the house where the couple had disappeared. How many customs did her kind have that she knew nothing about? Even if they didn't stay, she hoped to learn something more.

The leather soles of her boots slid a little on the polished stone in the corridor as they followed Roberts. Alaric stayed at her side, ready to keep her from falling. One entire wall of the hallway was lined with windows set into arches, reflecting the afternoon sun onto the paintings and tapestries lining the opposite wall. Chairs and benches sat under the windows, with a pair of tall doors standing at the opposite end. The benches near the doors were filled with a variety of well-dressed individuals. They stood and stared at them as they walked by. Glad the shirt she'd put on last night was marginally clean, Fin nervously tried to smooth some of the strands of her hair that had escaped the confines of her braid. "You're beautiful. Even if they don't see it," Alaric whispered in her ear.

Roberts stopped in front of the doors and addressed a man in a different uniform. "Captain Roberts requesting admittance. We're expected."

The man looked them over. "Armed? That is not normal."

Fin cringed at the withering look Roberts shot the man. "I don't care what you think is normal. I was told to present them as soon as we arrived. So, open the damn door and announce us."

Swallowing hard, the man jerked the door open. Stepping inside, he called out, "Your Majesty, Captain Roberts and...guests." He stepped aside and Fin followed Roberts into the throne room.

The room wasn't huge by any means, but it was cold. Impersonal. The columns were made to impress visitors, looming up and disappearing into a domed ceiling. About a dozen people milled around in small groups. Conversation stopped as they walked into the chamber. Fin's skin crawled under their scrutiny.

"Roberts! You're back!" A deep voice called out. Fin looked for the sound and found it.

King Christoph sat on a gilded chair high on a platform. Five wide steps, all carpeted in deep red, led up to the man. He was young, perhaps her age, and handsome. Brown hair peeked out from underneath a jewel-encrusted crown. He rose and started down the steps to greet them.

Roberts tried to bend his knee, but the King waved him off. Embracing him, he laughed. "Missed you, my friend. I take it the trip was worth it?" He looked past Roberts at her and her friends.

"My liege, I present your guests." Roberts drew breath, but stopped as the King moved in front of Gwen.

"Gwen of Lorien. I know you by reputation. And I know better than to offer, but my sword is yours if you need me to defend your honor." He smiled and bowed at her before moving on.

"Emile the Nimble. Should I hand over the key to my treasury now?"

Emile smiled, "No, not yet, Your Majesty. I'll let you know if you need to tighten security later."

Christoph laughed. "Trystian. I know not where you hail from, but we have heard tales of your skill in battle. I would never wish to fight against you."

Trystian bowed slightly at the compliment as the king moved on to the next in line.

"Alaric, the Islander. Your aim is legendary, my friend. I would be honored to shoot with you one day during your visit."

At last, he stopped in front of her. "And here she is. Serafina the Lost. The one who escaped and will lead her people to freedom." His tone was questioning.

"I prefer the name of Fin, Your Majesty. And I do not know that I am lost, or who you may believe me to be." She kept her voice firm. Now was not a time to show doubt and she knew it.

A slight smile crossed his face. "As you wish. Fin. We will talk about this tomorrow, you and I. Few Amari live this long without being caught. That alone distinguishes you from others."

"I've remained free because my companions would not have it otherwise." She looked him straight in the eyes. "And few Amari know their parents. This does not make me the one you seek."

He nodded. "Tomorrow, we will talk. For now, rest. Eat. Matters of state call my attention." He stepped back slightly. "Roberts, make sure they're well taken care of." He turned his back to them and went back to his throne.

"This way," Roberts' voice was low. He led them out of the room and down a smaller passageway.

"How'd he know us so well?" Fin whispered.

"Something tells me he had help." Gwen's voice had an edge to it.

Emile coughed before speaking. "Whoever does his intelligence gathering is good. I haven't heard that name for a long time. Not for the last ten years, anyway."

"None of us have, Emile." Alaric said. "Once we agreed to protect Fin, we let go of our past lives. He'd have to dig deep to find it."

Roberts stopped in front of some double doors. Opening them, he motioned for them to follow him.

A long table dominated the room, with about a dozen chairs around it. The polished floor was covered with ornate rugs in blue and gold. Five identical doors, each with someone standing next to it, lined the room.

"Here you are. The attendants are here for whatever you might need. Each room is identical. They'll bring you some dinner in about an hour or two I imagine. I'll leave you to your rest." He turned around and left, closing the door behind him.

"Fin, take the…" Trystian started to speak.

"I know, I know. The center room is mine." She moved across the room to the farthest door.

The attendant dropped a curtsey as she approached. She couldn't have been much more than twelve. And she was an Amari.

"None of that, please. I'm nothing special." Fin kept her voice low. She opened the door to her room. The girl followed her in, shutting the door behind her.

The room was larger than she'd ever slept in before. A small seating area, with a fireplace, made for a good place to relax. Near the fire was a bookcase with a few books. Fin did know how to read, but rarely had books at her disposal. Two massive columns led up two steps to an alcove where the bed sat. A steaming copper tub was off to the side, inviting her.

As Fin walked into the alcove, she fingered the heavy drapes that could close off the area from the seating area. Trystian would want someone to sit up all night on guard duty, but the curtains would give her some sense of privacy.

"We've sent your clothing off to be washed. I hope you don't mind. They looked like they needed it. My mother works in that part of the keep. She'll have them back by morning, I promise." Fin jumped slightly at the girl's voice. She'd forgotten she was in the room.

"Thank you. Is your mother an Amari as well?" Fin ran a hand over the bed linens. They were softer than anything she'd ever slept on.

"Both my parents are. His Majesty assigned me to your room for that reason. He thought you'd be more comfortable with me."

Fin smiled at her. "I suppose I am, though I've rarely been around other Amari. What's your name?"

The girl grinned. "It's Andra. Mother says it was the name of the last Queen of the Amari. But I don't feel very royal."

"Well, I like it. But I'd really like to get into that tub right now." Fin hoped the girl would take the hint and leave. She really had no idea how to send her away.

"Do you need my help? Mother said you'd been scarred recently and I should help you if you needed it." Andra swallowed hard.

Fin sighed. "No, I'm fine Andra. I can manage fine. Why don't you go see if you can get an idea when they'll bring us some food? I'm famished."

Andra left, thankfully. It was slow going, but Fin eventually got out of her clothes and into the steaming tub. Her hand still gave her difficulty. The hot water felt wonderful, though. After she got herself thoroughly scrubbed, she leaned back and tried to relax.

"Is it helping?" Gwen's voice startled Fin. Her body jerked awake, splashing water from the tub.

Gwen sat on the corner of the bed. Her damp hair was hanging loose. "The water. Is it helping your scar?"

Fin took a deep breath. "You scared me half to death!"

"You were asleep. I figured you could use it, but then food arrived. Decided you might need that more."

The water was cooler, but her arm did feel better. "Yes, it helped. I didn't know I'd fallen asleep." She grabbed the side of the tub to get ready to stand. Her left hand was still a little shaky, but most of the strength had returned.

Gwen rose to give her a hand. Fin grabbed one of the towels set out on a small tray near the tub. "I think we all napped some. We wouldn't have, if we weren't so exhausted. The beds are very comfortable here." She ran a hand down Fin's back. "Do you want some company tonight?"

Fin smiled back at her. "No, I need to think." She ran the towel down one of her legs. "Everybody slept? At once? That surprises me."

"Everyone but Alaric. He bathed, then parked himself outside the door to your room." She smiled at Fin. "He's doing very good at pretending you two are involved."

Fin blushed. "I'm sure it's part of the act. Who knows who might be spying on us now." Even if she wished it was real, she didn't dare think he might feel the same way.

With Gwen's help, Fin managed to get dressed again without a struggle. "They know you have the scar, Fin. Why not show it to them?" Gwen asked as Fin finished pulling on her boots.

"It's hard to explain. It's not like I got it in some honorable way during a duel or something. I got it because of what I did." Fin's voice trailed off. It would be a long time before she'd stop paying that price.

"Fin, you protected yourself. You did what needed to be done. If you hadn't done that, you'd be in chains and we'd be dead."

Sighing, she gave up the fight. Gwen was right but that didn't help. "The scars go much deeper than what you see on the skin. When Amari kill by using magic, it scars their very soul. We love in a way few could comprehend, and grieve the same way. It's why so many who are in captivity die. If forced to use magic for death and destruction, it kills you. Quickly, mercilessly, but not painlessly."

"Come on, let's get some food before Trystian eats it all." Gwen jumped down the steps and motioned for Fin to follow her.

Chapter Five

Fin lounged on the divan, absently sipping at the glass of wine in her hand as she watched the fire slowly die down. Her nose wrinkled slightly as she caught another whiff of her shirt. Andra had insisted that her clothing would be returned by dawn. She needed to make sure this outfit went next.

A light rap at her door startled her. It was late, and had been quiet for hours. Everyone else had gone to bed after dinner.

"Fin, are you awake? It's me." Alaric's low voice carried through the heavy door.

Pushing her hand through her hair, she rose and crossed the room to open the door. Alaric darted in, and she closed it behind him.

"Couldn't sleep. I think my body's too used to being up early to spend it sleeping now." She motioned towards one of the chairs in the room before curling up on the divan again. It wasn't a lie. She'd slept some, but woke up after a few hours. The quiet of the room unsettled her.

Alaric laughed. "I must be in the same predicament. We're so used to being on watch at this time of night-" his voice trailed off.

The silence dragged on. Fin's stomach was tied in knots. It was the first time they'd ever truly been alone together. There had always someone nearby.

She looked over the rim of her glass, truly seeing him for the first time. His long brown hair wasn't pulled back like it was on the road. She found herself thinking of running her hands through it.

"You're blushing!" He teased her. "What in the world are you thinking of?"

Sputtering, she put her wine glass down. "It's the wine. I must've had more than I realized." She prayed he bought her excuse.

Alaric sighed, stretching his long legs out towards the fire. "If we're going to be up anyway, want to start learning a little hand to hand combat?"

She arched an eyebrow. "And just what's so terribly wrong with me doing what I've done so far? I'm not much of an archer even, let alone a real fighter."

"There's nothing wrong with that, it's just...well..." He paused. "Let's face it. There will be more like we encountered a few days ago. I don't want to turn around and see you being dragged off in chains. You need to learn how to defend yourself without resorting to exposing who you are."

"That was a fluke. He caught me by surprise. I'll get a dagger from Emile for next time. He's got a few that aren't iron or steel I think." Her voice shook. *Damn*, she thought. She didn't want him knowing how scared she really was.

His features softened, "I don't want to ever see you in chains. You scared me the other day. When I saw him charging you, I thought I'd lost you." The look he gave her sent shivers down her spine.

"You really don't think I know how to defend myself?" She teased him, desperate to change the serious nature of the conversation. Rising gracefully, she challenged him. "Try me."

Alaric flew up from the chair he sat in, reaching out to grab her. With a squeal, she deftly stepped aside and put the divan between them. The chase was on!

She successfully evaded him for several minutes, alternately taunting him when he'd miss and laughing with triumph when she'd escape whatever hold he put her in.

Eventually, she found herself pinned against one of the stone columns separating the sleeping alcove from the sitting room. Her chest heaved as she caught her breath. Alaric's arms were wrapped around her, holding her by the wrists and pinning her body to the column with his own muscular frame.

She licked her lips as he touched her forehead with his own. He was breathing as hard as she was.

"Just how do you think you can get out of this one?" His voice was barely more than a whisper, sending chills down her spine.

The intensity in his eyes took her by surprise, and she found it hard to keep focus on them. "Oh, I've got a few more tricks up my sleeve."

The knot in her stomach grew even more. She'd imagined for weeks what it would be like to kiss him. If she didn't do it now, she never would. Hesitantly, she stretched upward and brushed her lips against his.

The feel of his lips made her heart race even faster. She pulled back, meeting his eyes again. Surprise and desire played across his face. She closed her eyes and met his kiss with one of her own.

He released her wrists and moved his hands to cradle her head. The kiss continued, turning the knot into passion. Her hands flew to his waist, frantically pulling his shirt out of his breeches. Her fingers worked their way underneath the cloth, finding his skin.

A low moan escaped him as she caressed his chest. She could feel his excitement building. He broke away, staring intently in her eyes. "Are you sure you want to do this?" he whispered.

In response, she slid one hand down the front of his breeches, stroking him lightly. "More than anything," she whispered back.

His lips came crashing down on hers again as he encircled her waist with his arms. As he raised her, she wrapped her legs around his waist. She moved her mouth toward his neck as he carried her towards the bed.

She sat on the bed where he placed her, watching as he pulled his shirt off. Her fingers lightly traced the outline of his muscles. Slowly, she inched her way down his chest to the top of his breeches. There was no turning back now. She unbuttoned them, sliding them down his legs to fall forgotten on the floor.

Before she could do anything more, he pulled her upright. "My turn," he whispered. "I want to see just how beautiful you are." He pulled her shirt off in one motion. Kissing her slowly, he caressed her body. By the time he was pulling off her breeches, she was barely able to stand.

Alaric paused just long enough to close the curtains to the alcove.

* * * *

Fin slept next to him. Alaric watched the steady rhythm of her breathing. Small, pale scars formed an interesting landscape across her body in the first light of dawn. The hour spent touching her had flown by. He'd wanted her for the better part of the last three years, willingly taking on the role of protector just to remain close to her. That Emile would've slit his throat to keep Alaric silent and Fin safe was something he could appreciate.

Emile. Damn. The man was a father figure to Fin. Sighing, Alaric slowly eased his way out of the bed. Until he knew more of how Fin felt, he couldn't risk Emile's wrath. The pretending was one thing. That was to keep James at bay. Facing the thief without her by his side wasn't a risk he was willing to take.

As quietly as he could, he pulled on his trousers and drew his shirt over his head. He wanted nothing more than to stay there, watch her wake up. Taking one long look at Fin's slumbering form, he grabbed his boots and slipped through the curtain.

Easing the knob on the door, he surveyed the common area. No one was there. Alaric darted through the door, pausing to shut it behind him, then made a beeline for his room. It was only one door down, though that was more by luck than design. Trystian and Gwen had the outer rooms, and he and Emile had chosen to flank Fin's room. He'd just shut the door to his room behind him when he heard another one open.

"Is everything alright, sir?"

Alaric jumped at the voice. Turning, he saw the man assigned to his room peeking out from his sleeping alcove. "Ah, yes. I just had to visit the-" Damn. What do nobles call the outhouse?

The attendant didn't look concerned. "Of course," he replied. "Your laundry has been returned. I put it into the cupboard for you. If you would like me to wait, I can take the ones you're wearing."

Just wanting the man to leave, Alaric quickly peeled off his shirt and trousers. "Will breakfast be brought soon?" he asked, as he moved to find his clean clothing.

"I believe so, sir. The others will be arriving soon with the rest of the clothing. I have to go help with the food." He carefully draped Alaric's dirty clothes over his arm and left.

Alaric stopped, leaning his head against the wood of the armoire in relief as he heard the door close. Too close. He drew a deep breath. He could walk out now and no one would know.

He found his favorite shirt, a deep green linen, and pulled it on. Tucking it into his black trousers, he started to think of his next steps. If he could get back into Fin's room with only the group finding him, then they could play up he spent the night in there. And maybe he could still be the one to wake her up.

A smile played across his lips. Yeah, he wanted to wake her up. Every day for the rest of his life if she'd let him.

Leaving his boots on the floor, he ran a hand through his hair briefly before walking back out to the common room.

Trystian and Gwen were up, sitting at the large table. "How'd you sleep?" the huge man asked.

"Better than I would've thought," Alaric answered. "I thought I'd be up all night at first. Kept expecting someone to come charging into the room." He pulled out a chair and sat. "What about you two?"

"It took some time, but I think we were too tired to fight it long. And the bed was far more comfortable than the ground." Gwen had her short sword out on the table in front of her.

"Any sign that Fin or Emile are awake yet?"

Trystian shrugged. "I woke up when the fool with my clothes showed up. He didn't like that my armor was on the floor. If that wasn't enough, me charging out with my sword drawn gave him more incentive to get the hell out."

"He's just doing his job, Tryst. No reason to make him rethink his career path." Gwen rubbed at her blade with a soft cloth and some oil.

Alaric drew breath to reply, but the doors leading to the common area opened wide. Five people came in, each carrying a tray that smelled amazing. Three were placed in the front of them, while two more attendants walked toward Emile and Fin's rooms. He recognized one as the girl assigned to Fin. Jumping up, Alaric intercepted her. "I'll take it." He eased the tray from her hands.

The girl smiled back at him, "Thank you, sir. The tray's heavy." She opened the door for him.

The curtains were still shut. The girl darted past, parting the drapes for him. The early morning light filtered through the colored glass in the windows. Fin still slept, her back to him. "I'll relight the fire," she whispered as she scooped up the discarded clothing on the floor. "I didn't want to wake her earlier, so I put her clothing over there."

She pointed to a small pile sitting on a side table. With that, the girl disappeared through the drapes.

Alaric placed the tray on the floor near the bed. Carefully, he sat on the bed and reached over to stroke Fin's hair. She stirred, rolling toward him, still asleep. He leaned over to kiss her, then stopped. The fresh scar, visible in the light, drew his attention. No wonder she'd been in so much pain! He'd remembered enough last night not to touch her arm, but had no idea how extensive the mark was.

"Do I look that horrible in the morning?" Fin murmured.

Glancing down, he smiled. "No, you don't. You're beautiful." He leaned in to kiss her gently.

The sound of the door opening and closing reminded him of the girl. "Our company's gone." He kissed her again, a deep lingering one.

She sighed and snuggled up against his chest. "No fair. You got dressed."

A deep chuckle rose from his throat. "Clean clothes, even. You might want to try it."

"Maybe. In a bit. Right now, I want to think about where those wonderful smells are coming from."

"I brought you food." He kissed her on the head, then moved to retrieve the tray. Placing it on the bed, "I left mine out on the table. Hope you don't mind sharing."

She lifted the silver dome covering the tray, surveying the contents underneath. "There's more food here than I could eat in a day. Sharing just became mandatory."

His stomach growled. "You win," he said with a grin.

Chapter Six

Fin lay curled up, her head in Alaric's lap, content. "I don't think I've eaten that much in years," she giggled. "Sure feels good to have a full stomach for a change."

Alaric's fingers combed through her tangled mass of hair. It felt so good, sitting next to him in bed. Natural. "True. Though I don't think you should say that around Emile too much. He does try to make what we find edible."

She smiled. "True enough. I'd hate for him to start getting exotic and forget that the plant he's using causes more discomfort than flavor!"

"Does your arm still hurt?"

For a moment, Fin considered hiding her arm under the sheets. After the night they'd just had, though, she knew he'd seen all her scars. "Not as much as it did. I can hold things now. It's going to take a lot of time to heal, though." Her voice drifted off. How could she explain the pain that marked her very soul?

The feel of his lips on her shoulder warmed her, pushing aside the memories. She shifted, making it so she could look him in the face. "Alaric, last night was all I could've asked for from you. And I want to tell you-"

His finger touched her lips, silencing her, his dark brown eyes holding her attention. "Shh. Me first. I've wanted you since I laid eyes on you. The last three years have changed that. I don't just want you. I love you."

Fin's entire body trembled at his words. "I'm not an easy person to love, Alaric. But you're more than a friend to me as well. I don't know what the future holds for me, but I know I'd be devastated if I couldn't share every second with you." She leaned forward, her forehead touching his. "I love you, too."

His hands cradled her head as they kissed. Fin pressed her naked body closer against him, her hands working up under his tunic to caress his skin as the kiss deepened. His lips left hers, traveling down her neck. Fin gasped for air, anticipating the passion to come.

"You can't go in there!" Trystian's voice boomed loud through her chambers.

Fin's head snapped towards the curtained area. She felt Alaric's muscles tense up.

"You are in no position to make demands of me," James' voice wasn't pleasant. "I'm here to see Her Highness, and you *will* get out of my way or be removed!"

The tray of dishes from their breakfast clattered to the floor as Alaric moved from the bed. "Get dressed, but take your time. I'll stall him out there."

Fin nodded, sliding out from the sheets. The curtains barely made a sound as he left the room. She kept her back to them, trying to make sense of the pile of clean clothing.

"Good morning, James. I trust you slept well?" Alaric's deep voice was deliberately friendly. Fin was willing to bet he was making sure James got the impression Alaric was here all night.

Fin finally found the shirt and trousers she was looking for. A deep brown set with just a hint of green embroidery around the sleeves. Nothing fancy, but King Christoph had said he'd want to talk to her today. This would pass. At least the breeches hadn't been patched more than once.

"His Majesty wishes to speak with Her Highness now. I'm here to escort her." Fin didn't know how he did it, but James had a manner of speaking that made her jaw clench.

"Fine. She's getting dressed. I'm sure we'll be ready shortly." Alaric was keeping things casual. At least, that's what it sounded like. As far as she knew, those two were staring each other down.

"You didn't hear me, Islander." There was no mistaking the scorn in James' voice now. "She's the only one that was summoned. You four stay here, and await King Christoph's will. Though I wouldn't bother unpacking. I'm sure you won't be staying much longer."

Fin had heard enough. Hurriedly tucking in the last of her shirt, she grabbed a leather tie off the floor and darted out to the common room. "Then I'll be sure to convey our regards to him for his hospitality while we talk today. I would hate to leave without him knowing it was appreciated, if brief." Her hands deftly worked her hair into a braid as she looked around the room.

Alaric lounged in one of the chairs, his long legs stretched toward the fire. Trystian, Gwen, and Emile all stood behind James. Their expressions ranged from amused to furious. James, however, gave her a look that sent chills down her spine.

"If you're ready--" James held out his arm to escort her.

Fin stepped down and leaned over Alaric, planting a kiss on his cheek. "I'll be back soon. Don't miss me too much." She made sure her voice was loud enough for James to hear.

Alaric's response, though was for her ears only. "Watch your back. I don't like you going to see this King alone. Or his escort."

She nodded, then straightened. "Well, let's not keep His Majesty waiting." Deliberately, she ignored the proffered arm and strode out the door.

Eight armed guards waited in the hallway outside the common area, surrounding her and James as soon as they emerged. "You should reconsider your allegiances," James said as they walked. "There are plenty of Amari men here who would willingly help you adjust to our way of life. There's so few of us left. It would be a shame not to keep the bloodline pure."

Swallowing her retort, she kept her eyes on the guard leading them. His brusque manner brought out the worst in her. Choking the life out of James before she got to the King would be out of the question. "I'm not royalty, James. The idea of a pure bloodline descending from me, or marrying for power, doesn't apply. I will marry whom I choose."

James' back stiffened at her words, and his face grew stern. "You *are* my Queen, Lady Serafina. Even if you don't see it yet. And an Amari Queen needs to have an Amari King."

The guard in front of her stopped before a plain wooden door. Another guard opened the door, and she was motioned inside.

The room was warm, inviting. Lined with bookshelves neatly stacked with books and scrolls, the room beckoned her to relax. A small fireplace in one wall, with windows on each side, kept the chill off. A couple of cushioned chairs, upholstered in leather the same dark hue as the wood, sat near enough to the hearth to maximize the comfort. King Christoph stood near them, his hand resting on the mantle. "Ah, Lady Fin. So glad you could join me." He smiled at her, waving a hand toward one of the chairs. "Please, have a seat."

"Thank you," she replied, easing into one of the chairs. She couldn't relax, though. Not with James standing behind her chair.

She watched as Christoph moved toward a side table with a decanter and some glasses. "Can I interest you in something to drink?"

"No, I'm fine. Thank you for asking." Damn. She couldn't keep her voice steady.

Christoph turned to her, smiling. "You can relax, Lady Fin. There are no chains in this room, hidden or otherwise." He poured himself a drink, then settled into the chair opposite of her. "If you're that concerned, I'm surprised that you didn't take me up on my offer this morning."

"What offer?" Fin's stomach plummeted. Something was very wrong here.

"I told James that any of your companions were welcome to come with you." He leaned forward, keeping his hands where she could see them. "I'm rather surprised none of them chose to. It's rare for an Amari to travel the world for as long as you have and trust a stranger this quickly."

"Your Majesty, we were told--" she shot a withering glance up at James, "--that I was being summoned and that my companions were not allowed to come."

Christoph leaped to his feet. All sense of friendliness left his face. "That is *not* what I instructed." The King looked past her, his focus shifted to James. "Guards!" he commanded.

The door opened, admitting four armed men. "Yes, Your Majesty?" The man who spoke was the one she'd focused on during her walk here.

"Daniels, go to the guest quarters and invite *all* of our guests to meet with us here. And be quick about it. I don't want them to fear I'd hurt Lady Fin."

The soldier turned on his heels and dashed from the room. Christoph never changed his focus. "James, explain to me why you disobeyed my instructions." There was no question in his voice. Only the demand of an answer.

"If Her Majesty wishes to discuss Amari matters, then only an Amari should be present to give counsel." James replied.

"I am not your Queen!" Fin shot up from her chair, livid. "Get that through your head!"

Christoph held up a hand to silence her. "Whether or not she is the woman you believe her to be, James, I am still your King. You swore fealty to me when you took my offer of sanctuary. Perhaps you're rethinking your loyalties now." He motioned to the guards. "Escort him back to his home. We will discuss this further at a later time."

James wrested his arm away from the guard. His flushed face scared Fin even more. His gold eyes stared at her as he was removed from the room. She waited until the door shut behind him before taking a deep breath. Her entire body shook. "Your Majesty, I think I want that drink after all."

"Of course. And, please, call me Christoph. The whole royal thing is more of a pain than I ever imagined. When I'm relaxed and around friends, I prefer to know they're my friends and not someone trying to gain favor." He poured Fin her drink and handed it to her before sitting down again. "Daniels is a good man. He'll bring your friends here soon enough."

Fin sank back into her chair and sipped. "Thank you for that. I wonder why James didn't simply tell us we were all welcome."

Christoph leaned back in his chair. "He's a good man, don't get me wrong. Roberts sees him as a son in some ways, trusts him quite a bit. And I trust Roberts. James though…he's got some ideas that border on radical."

"How so?" Fin knew she shouldn't ask, but she couldn't help herself.

"What I'm trying to do within my borders is pretty radical, at least in comparison to the other kingdoms. I don't think the Amari should be slaves. Magic may be limited to your race, but the cost is high. Too high, if you ask me. Forcing them to endure that intensity of pain so you don't lose some sheep to a coyote? That's wrong. No one should live in chains." He grew quiet.

"Your father didn't feel the same way."

"No, he didn't," Christoph sighed. "He was a good man in several ways. And he treated the Amari he kept better than most do. But magic isn't something you control by threats and beatings. Every Amari I've ever met only wants to live in peace. Live their lives, raise their families, grow their crops, be happy. Few of you actively use your powers, and only in a time of need. You don't coax the crops to grow, but you make sure your children can last a lean winter if the harvest yield was small. If anything, you have a greater appreciation of life and death, of how we interact with each other and the earth beneath our feet, than any other race. I'm envious of that."

A small pop caught Fin's attention. Glancing to her right, she saw a woman with red hair emerge from behind one of the bookcases. "Lyssa! You made it!" Christoph moved across the room, embracing the stranger. He draped one of his arms across her shoulders, leading her towards Fin.

"Lyssa, it is my great honor to introduce you to Fin. Fin, this is my wife, Lyssa."

Fin rose from her chair, intent on making some semblance of a bow, and stopped short when she saw the woman's gold eyes.

Lyssa smiled, "Yes, Fin. I'm Amari. Most don't know. Even Christoph's father was fooled." She glanced at Christoph, her face beaming. "He'd never have agreed to the marriage if he knew otherwise." Her attention shifted back to Fin. "Even now, most in the keep itself don't know. When I go out in public, my eyes are green." She blinked, and her eye color shifted.

"Why not reveal yourself, though? Surely you're safe enough in your own home." Fin asked, more confused that the woman still felt the need to hide even here.

She shrugged, "The ruse was so normal by the time we met, it's second nature to me. Even now, you shade your eyes as I do. How many would come for me, question

Christoph's rule, if they knew? The world is not ready for an Amari Queen."

Fin nodded. She understood. "You might want to let James know that. He's obsessed with the idea." The words came out far more sarcastically than she thought they would.

Alarm flickered across Lyssa's beautiful face. Glancing up at Christoph, she whispered, "James?"

"He was on the patrol with Roberts when Fin and her companions were found. I've got him on house arrest. He won't be any further problem."

Fin's curiosity was piqued. Something about James frightened Lyssa. Before she could ask any further questions, the door opened to the library, admitting Daniels and her companions.

All three visibly relaxed when they saw Fin. Alaric moved up behind her, whispering, "Everything okay?"

Fin nodded in response. She'd fill them all in later. But not here, not now.

Christoph clapped his hands together, regaining her attention. "So, who's up for a walk through town?"

Chapter Seven

Alaric shifted in the bed, cradling Fin's naked body next to his. The steady rise of her chest reassured him. The dream hadn't been specific. But it scared him enough to wake up and make sure she still slept next to him.

This place was either everything their host claimed it was, or a very good front. The entire day was spent trying to put Fin and himself at ease. He wasn't sure about the rest, but he was dangerously close to being convinced it was real. If he and Fin had a future together, he couldn't imagine it being anywhere else. She could finally be who she was born to be without fear.

The barely audible click of a doorknob turning startled him. There, he heard it again. Placing a hand over Fin's mouth, he whispered, "someone's here" into her ear. Her head turned to meet his gaze. Silently, he held one finger to his lips, then motioned over his shoulder to the other room.

He watched her roll off the bed, grabbing at a shirt lying across the foot. His hands found his breeches and he shoved his legs into them quickly. Rising from the bed, he turned to face Fin again. "Stay here until I know what's going on," he spoke in hushed tones, not wanting to alert anyone else that he was awake.

She crouched near the edge of the bed, nodding. She knew the drill, but his stomach still plummeted. Living in fear like she did was no life.

He peeked through the curtains, surveying the room. The fire still burned, and there wasn't enough furniture in there to make hiding easy. Hushed speaking out in the common room drew his attention. Crossing the room, he cocked his head to one side and placed an ear against the door. Emile was out there, and Trystian. The other voices, though, he couldn't distinguish.

Cautiously, he opened the door a crack and peered outside. Gwen was pacing. Something was wrong. He stepped outside, shutting the door behind him.

Emile's head snapped around, giving Alaric a calculated look. Three armed men were in the room, along with the King and Queen. From the looks of everyone, they'd just been awakened.

"Alaric. There you are." Gwen let out a long breath. "Fin's okay, right?"

"Yeah, she's asleep." He looked at everyone, puzzled. "What going on?"

"James attacked the guards watching his quarters," Christoph replied. "We were concerned that he might--"

Fin's voice, screaming in panic, shattered the silence. Alaric cursed himself for leaving her alone as he ran back toward her room. Throwing the door open, he screamed, "Fin!" as he leapt up the small steps leading to the sleeping alcove. He shoved the curtains aside. The room was empty. She wasn't there.

"Over there!" Emile pointed towards a spot in the wall. The edge wasn't lining up quite right. The two darted over. Alaric tried prying it open with his fingers while Emile ran his hands over the wall nearby. "There has to be a trigger of some kind," he insisted.

Fin screamed again, the sound muffled. Panic flared in Alaric, and he drew back slightly. Ramming his bare shoulder into the spot, he tried to break through the hidden door with brute strength. He stepped back to do it again, just as Emile found the right location. The door flew open and his momentum drove him forward. "Fin!" He shouted her name into the dark tunnel.

He could hear movement ahead. He began to run, not caring what was in front of him. His heart pounded with fear. He had to find her.

Something dug into his shoulder. Grunting in pain, he pushed forward. A faint blue light began to illuminate the tunnel. The sound of Fin's voice as she struggled with her abductor drove him forward.

One final corner and he saw her. James was restraining her as they stood, bathed in an iridescent light. Alaric lunged forward, reaching out for her hand. His fingertips brushed against hers as her image began to fade. "If you call," he choked out.

"You will come," she replied. Her face, terrified, disappeared.

Alaric slumped to the ground. He'd failed her. He was supposed to protect her, damn it! How can he save her when he has no idea where she'd been taken?

"Alaric, wasn't that your favorite shirt that she was wearing?" Emile's voice, calm and calculating, sounded from his right. He looked up at the man who Fin saw as her father.

Emile nodded once. "Let's hope it's not cold where he took her." He looked down at Alaric. "We'll get her back. Somehow." He reached out a hand.

Alaric clasped it and rose. "That we will," he vowed.

Christoph and Lyssa walked around the area where Fin had disappeared. "Get Roberts in here. And wake up Murielle. She's the only one who would know what this is," he ordered.

Lyssa looked up and met Alaric's gaze. "Everyone should leave here. We'll talk in the common room. Murielle will need space to figure out what this is, and you," she pointed at Alaric, "need to have your shoulder looked at."

Alaric looked at his right shoulder. Slivers of wood jutted out from several places. It didn't hurt, though. The pain of losing Fin was far more real.

Emile nudged Alaric forward and he followed everyone out of the tunnel.

Back in the common room, he ignored everyone. Christoph was giving orders, making sure the other rooms were searched and getting torches in place down that dark tunnel. Absently, Alaric noted the walk out was much shorter than it'd seemed when he was chasing Fin. It was still cold, though.

He knew people were talking around him. Lyssa had asked for tweezers and had begun to pull the slivers from his skin. He didn't care. As far as he knew, someone was putting chains on Fin right now. The next time he saw her, she'd be broken.

"I don't think that's what he will do to her, Alaric." Lyssa's voice jarred him from the imagined horrors in his mind.

He jerked his head up, focusing on her face. She didn't look at him, but concentrated on his shoulder.

"James has worn chains before. He knows what it does to an Amari. He wants her to lead a rebellion. She can't do that while chained."

"Then why kidnap her? Why force her to go somewhere against her will?" Gwen's voice was subdued.

"He took her home." A new voice declared.

Alaric twisted in his chair, staring at the old woman who'd spoken. "Where is home?"

Murielle looked past him, her focus on Lyssa. "Home is Uamh nan Amari. It is where we lived before the last great reaping."

"The cave in the story?" Alaric asked, puzzled. "Why would he take her there?"

"It is where she came from. He believes that taking her there will remind her of who she is, of what she is supposed to do." Murielle paused. "Or, what he thinks she is destined to do."

Christoph spoke up, his voice even. "I know the way. My father was part of that raid, bragged about it for years. He thought he'd struck it rich and would be able to expand his lands because of the Amari that he chained after that night." He scanned the room. "We'll need to keep the force small. I don't want James to do something desperate if he sees an army coming his way. The four of you, me, and Roberts should be enough."

"I'm coming with you, Christoph." Lyssa finished with Alaric's shoulder and placed the tweezers on the table next to him.

"Lyssa, no, I won't allow you-"

With measured movements, she placed the tweezers back into the small travel roll of first aid supplies. "It doesn't matter what you allow, Christoph. If it wasn't for me, Fin would not be his captive now. She has spent her entire life keeping me safe. The least I can do is relieve her of this burden she didn't know she carried."

Alaric glanced at Christoph and back at Lyssa. "What are you talking about? What burden?"

Christoph ran a hand through his hair, "Lyssa, we've been through this. There's no reason to jeopardize your safety now. No one has to know."

"But I know, Christoph. Fin doesn't. It'd be one thing if she did and agreed, but she wasn't given that opportunity! I owe her that much!"

Trystian's deep voice cut through the growing tension in the room. "You're the one in the story. The long lost Queen."

Lyssa nodded, "Fin and I were born on the same day, but not to the same family. She was the one that my nursemaid took to the river. I was hidden as a non-Amari child. We had a few families that were both Amari and human, and the children took after their human parent. The hope was that they would be so busy trying to find Fin that

I would remain safe until the time was right to come forward."

"So, you let some child become hunted her entire life just so you could sleep warm at night?" Disgust dripped from Emile's voice.

"It wasn't like that, not for me. I wasn't given a choice, either. By the time Christoph came to the throne, I'd told him everything. We tried to find her, bring her here for her own safety. I hate the idea that she's been hunted, isolated from her own kind, because of a lie."

"Except now she's being held captive by some raving lunatic who thinks she's you." Alaric rose, pushing the chair away from him.

"I don't think he'll hurt her, Alaric. He wants something from her, something that he can't get by harming her."

Alaric glared at Lyssa, "He may not put chains on her or a whip to her back, but he'll still try to possess her, control her." He kept his eyes on her, "Let me know when it's time to go. I'm going to pack." He strode into his room, slamming the door behind him.

Chapter Eight

Fin slumped to the cold stone beneath her, her strength sapped. Whatever magic James had used made her weak, unable to stand.

"You'll be fine in a moment, Your Highness. The first time you travel like that it can be hard to adjust to. You'll get used to it soon enough." James' voice echoed from the enveloping darkness around her.

She almost protested over the title he used for her, but bit her tongue. *Stay calm, keep your eyes open, say nothing*, she told herself. It was one of the first lessons Emile had taught her on how to survive. Observe, calculate strengths and weaknesses, and only act when the odds were in your favor.

A torch flared to life. James stood to her left, holding it aloft. They were in a cave of some kind. Excitement danced across his face. "Welcome home, Your Highness." He held out his other hand to help her up.

Her stomach churned at the idea of touching him, but she took his hand anyway. Her legs threatened to give way beneath her, but held her weight. "What do you mean, home?" she asked, keeping her voice low.

James' face shone with an expression that bordered on fanatical. "This is Uamh nan Amari, Your Highness. The Cave of the Amari. This is where you lived for the first few years of your life. From here, you will lead our people to freedom."

Fin drew in a deep breath, her eyes trying to make out detail in the meager light the torch gave off. The walls revealed little. A bit of carving near the top of an archway leading somewhere, overturned and broken pieces of pottery strewn near the edges of the circular room. She shivered, rubbing her arms with her hands. The shirt she wore did little to combat the chill of the cavern. Alaric's shirt. The look on his face as she disappeared gave her hope. He wouldn't abandon her. All she had to do was call to him.

But how? She knew so little of what her race could do, or the way magic worked. She was untrained, undisciplined. Unless there was a need, she couldn't do anything.

But there is a need, she thought. She needed him with her. Wanted to have his arms around her, to feel that sense of safety that she'd never experienced before. Closing her eyes, she turned that need into a something concrete in her mind and willed it down into the earth below her.

A hand grabbed her elbow, breaking her concentration. "Enough. We need to find you something suitable to wear, and food. Tomorrow, after you're rested and acclimated to being home, the memories will return." James guided her forward into the darkness.

"How did we live down here, without daylight?" Fin asked. A dark cloud had settled over James' face, unsettling her. She didn't know if he knew she'd called out to Alaric, or recognized his shirt as what she wore. But she had to get him talking.

The corridor made a slight bend to the left. "Before we were forced out, the mountain welcomed us. It allowed us to grow crops, light fires for warmth and cooking, and would mimic the world above. Light would greet us at dawn, and lessen at sunset. And it will welcome us again. Once you have led us to freedom and our people have returned here, it will remember us, sustain us, as it did before."

She brushed her fingers lightly against the worked stone of the wall. It was cold, dead. It did not welcome her back. It still felt the pain of the raid that ripped the lives of the Amaris' lives to shreds.

The tunnel opened up to a giant cavern. Even in the meager torchlight, Fin could see outlines of houses, a central square. A waterfall, frozen, glittered against a wall. *Strange*, she thought, *it's not cold enough for water to freeze. Not like that.* The ghostly image of mist, forever locked into place as it arose from the lake below the falls, made her heart ache.

"We go there," James spoke, pointing to a large series of buildings. "Your old rooms would be too small, but no one would mind if you took the Queen's chamber. It's yours, now." Suddenly, he dropped to a knee in front of her. The torch lay next to him, struggling to keep burning against the cold earth. "Welcome home, Your Majesty."

He grabbed her hands, formally kissing the back of each. Something tugged at the edge of her mind. Yes, this was home. She had lived here. But the pull was for a far humbler house than a palace.

She drew a steady breath. "Get up. It's cold, and I'm tired. Can't we just find someplace to rest first? I'm willing to bet the palace was looted by the invaders. I doubt there's anything left in there to help us." Silently, she prayed it made sense to him.

He nodded, "Your wisdom shines, Your Majesty. Come. We will see you secure for the night. I'll gather some supplies and we'll assess things tomorrow." He led her down the long staircase and into the dead city.

* * * *

Something was wrong. Fin could feel it. The heavy fog of sleep refused to budge, fighting her will to wake up. Was she drugged? James had eaten the same meal as she had when they settled into the small, abandoned house. She'd convinced him it was perfect because it was so small. Just two rooms. She would take the bedroom, with no windows, and he could sleep in the main area. The long, cushioned bench was more than big enough. He could even move it in front of the door if he felt safer. The city was abandoned; no one would come bother them in the night. They could light a fire, eat in peace, and get some undisturbed rest. So, why was it so hard for her to wake up?

With effort, she cleared her foggy mind enough to open her eyes slightly. James stood in the room, his back to her. The deep green cloth balled up in his left fist looked too familiar. She glanced under the blankets to see her naked body. He'd undressed her while she slept! Fear crept through her body. What else had he done to her?

"Rest assured, I did not do anything inappropriate. Merely removed *this*," he raised his hand. "You may have little regard to our ways, but that will change. I, on the other hand, will wait until the ceremony is complete."

"What ceremony?" Fin kept a firm grip on the covers over her.

James turned. His gold eyes held an edge of madness as he stared at her. "You're too young to remember, of course. We'll have to bring those memories back before we can move forward. So much time wasted with other races instead of being taught what it is to be Amari." He shifted, heading towards the door. "I found suitable clothing for you. It's on the chest in the corner. I'm burning this."

"James, stop! What ceremony are you talking about?"

He stopped, his hand poised to raise the latch to the door. "The one that was started when we were children, binding us together for life." He looked over his shoulder, raw hunger on his face.

She bolted upright on the bed, her hands still clutching the blankets around her. That's when she felt it. A small iron band around her ankle. Terrified, she stared at the man holding her captive. "You chained me? Why?"

His face twisted, disgust and hatred replacing the lust she'd just seen. Holding up Alaric's shirt, he replied, "You gave yourself up to someone like *him*, tried to ignore your duty to your people. You know nothing of what it means to be Amari! If this is what it takes to force you to remember who and what you are, do what is right, then so be it. I'll make you wear them for the next seventy years. You spent too many years among humans, my dear. It's time someone forced you to do what you must."

Fin stared at James as he turned around and left the room. He'd chained her, claimed ownership of her. And would force her to become the person he thought she was. Closing her eyes, she tried to call out to Alaric. The small band of metal flared with heat, searing her skin. Biting back a cry, she pulled back the covers to examine the area.

The anklet was barely an inch wide, and sealed shut. A thin layer of padding would ensure the iron didn't touch her skin, unless she used magic without permission. Even if she could've figured out the locking mechanism, her fingers wouldn't have withstood touching it for that long. The only time Emile had tried to show her how to pick a lock, just in case, it had burned her fingers so bad that she couldn't use them for weeks. And that hadn't been attached to her. This one was.

She rose from the bed, her mind a whirl of thoughts. She had to keep James happy. His entire bearing had changed since the night before. Had that been his plan the whole time? Lure her into thinking he wanted to protect her, elevate her to lead a revolution, only to enslave her to his own will? Limping slightly, she found the clothes he referred to. A blue linen underdress, with lacings at the side. The overdress was heavier, and trimmed in fur. Both showed obvious signs of wear, or neglect. She didn't dare walk around naked, though, so she donned the clothing. A pair of soft leather boots, lined in wool, were found. Just to be safe, she peeked inside each one to make sure no rats or mice had taken up residence.

Her fingers brushed against the band as she pulled a boot onto her left foot. She quickly pulled them from their task, sticking the singed fingertips in her mouth. Fear gripped her soul. She'd heard far too many stories told in inns, seen the corpses of Amari who had died from the wounds inflicted by the magic their masters had forced them to do. Emile and the others had sacrificed so much of their own lives to prevent her from this exact situation. She owed so much to them.

Despair washed over her. How would she be able to escape? James had put that on her. The only way it would come off is if he removed it, or was dead. Until then, he could force her to do anything his soul desired.

And that's what scared her the most.

Chapter Nine

Alaric fidgeted in his saddle. Maybe that wasn't the right word. Bristled sounded better in his head. The pace was too slow. He wanted to be there, find Fin. And slaughter James if he'd hurt even a single cell of her body.

"I understand, Alaric. This isn't easy on any of us." Emile spoke quietly as he rode beside him.

He sighed, "That obvious?"

Emile laughed softly, "For those of us trained to observe, yes. I knew how you felt about Fin within two days of us coming across you. Even as the fever still raged and Fin struggled to keep you alive. You were delirious, yes. But I still knew."

Alaric didn't trust himself to do more than nod in agreement.

"My only question now, Alaric, is if you're willing to take over?"

"Take over what?"

"Fin's safety, of course." Emile paused. "I'm not getting any younger, you know. Even found a few grey hairs the other day. What she needs most, I can't provide." He thrust a chin toward Trystian's back, a few yards ahead of them. "Trystian's not what she needs. And she loves you. You love her. The only problem I see is the aftermath."

"Aftermath?"

"When we part ways. With Trystian and Gwen, she'll accept them not being part of her daily life any more. Especially if the two of you stay with Christoph. He's a decent man, trying to do what's right. She needs to get off the road, Alaric. Stop running and have a chance at a normal life."

Alaric paused, "I'll agree with you there. But why can't you stay as well?"

The tired smile that passed over Emile's face worried Alaric. For the first time, he saw the other man's age. "It's not as easy as that, Alaric. Just promise me you're willing to take care of her from this point forward. I'm not hung up on the so-called morals of proper behavior. I've spent too much of my life in the world. Marriage is great, but that's between the two of you. I made a pledge a very long time ago, to care for her until someone who could do it more completely came into her life. It's your turn, if you're willing."

"There's nothing I'd rather do, my friend."

"Good. Glad that's settled. Now, we need to get some more information from that one." He glanced over his shoulder at Lyssa, riding behind them. "Think you can keep your anger in check? I know you're pissed, but don't hold it against her. She was just as much a child as Fin was. Neither of them had a choice in this."

Alaric clenched his jaw momentarily. "Fine. But I still think it was a lousy thing to do to Fin."

"I agree, Alaric." Lyssa's voice carried up to them.

He moved his horse to the side, giving her room to come up between him and Emile. "What really happened in the raid?"

She looked ahead, but her eyes weren't focused on the path. "I don't remember much, really. Fin and I were both only about three or five. Barely old enough to know our names, or why we needed to run." She paused, "I remember a lot of screaming, and someone kept telling me over and over to hide my eyes. I was slipped into a group of children, most of whom had a human parent. The cave wept for us, though."

Startled by her words, Alaric sat up in his saddle. "How can a cave weep for you?"

A wistful smile crossed her lips. "Uamh nan Amari was alive, Alaric. The earth beneath us now is how the Amari can do magic. We're connected to the natural energy around us in a very different way than humans are. This is why any harm we do hurts us. The earth does not take kindly to the altering of others. It's why we don't carry weapons that aren't made of silver or other natural metals, and must obey anyone who chains us. The mixture used to create iron and steel severs our connection with the energy around us. It weighs down on us, forcing us to do things we find abhorrent just in the hope that the connection is regained. The only thing we cannot be forced to do is lie."

She turned, her eyes fluctuating between green and gold. "This is why I believe James won't chain her, Alaric. He knows how that feels, to have that connection ripped from your soul. The more metal placed around us, on us, the more desperate we become. To be Amari is to be connected to the world. When we were enslaved that day, the cave wept with us."

"The thing I don't understand is why he'd take her there to begin with," Christoph rode up on Alaric's right. "Several Amari went back after I took the throne. Two months later, they returned. Reported the settlement was dead. The mountain had remained cold for them."

"He took her there because it's an image in his mind, a symbol of what we once were. He sees only the past, not the future." A shadow crossed Lyssa's face, alarming Alaric. "We need to hurry, Christoph. He has started something. I can feel it. And the ground is not accepting of it. I fear for more than just Fin now."

Alaric dug his heels into his horse's side, urging it to gallop. The forest blurred past him as the mountain drew him closer. Fin called to him, he'd felt it. Back in his room, before they left. And he'd felt it urging him forward all morning.

Until now.

Chapter Ten

Fin stumbled, her weary feet barely able to go another step. All day long, James had dragged her from place to place, insisting she had been in each place before. Telling her she'd played in one field, or swam in a pool. Constantly commanding her to remember the scene he painted before her.

And she would remember, on occasion. Only it wasn't the scene he described. He wanted her to remember events, and all she could do is recall watching them. A royal procession through the streets? Yes, she'd remembered that. But as a young girl perched on her father's shoulder, not the Princess gliding past and waving to the people. Giving out gifts on a feast day? No, she received one.

The bands kept coming, too. Each time she failed to remember what he instructed, told him she saw it differently, a new iron band was latched around her arm or leg. The weight made it almost impossible to keep pace with James, yet his commands compelled her to obey. She was so tired, couldn't he see that?

She fell, her hands scraping on the loose pieces of cobblestone. He didn't look back at her. Maybe he would finally let her rest.

Light flared ahead of her. She raised her head, shielding her eyes from the brightness. James walked around a huge courtyard, lighting torches that stood around the perimeter. She remembered this place.

A boy, almost a man, stood in the center. Two girls, both young and with red hair, played with each other nearby. They could've been twins, except for how they were dressed. Fin drew in a sharp breath. One of them was her.

An older couple were talking with the boy. He was human, dark hair, thin build. At least, he looked human. As the memory progressed, she saw him shift. His eyes shone gold. He was Amari.

And he was Emile.

The younger Emile knelt before the couple, swearing some vow between their hands. Fin watched her younger self try to listen to what was being said.

"Get in here."

James' demanding voice broke through the vision. The skin beneath the bands of iron recoiled as they warmed up when she didn't respond instantly. Struggling to rise, she responded with a weak, "I'm coming."

He moved toward her, roughly pulling her forward by her arm. Fin struggled to get her feet under her as he dragged her towards the center.

"This is your last chance. I don't know how you can keep lying to me, but I promise you I'll keep piling the chains on until you stop." He growled at her, impatience warring with anger on his face.

"I'm not lying, James. I can't. The bands won't let me. Just take some of them off, they're too heavy." Fin whispered.

The weight was too much to bear. She couldn't stand any more. Her soul cried out for the connection to the world around her that'd been all but blocked out.

"You and I stood here, as children. Our families surrounded us. The entire city came to watch the ceremony. We didn't have to say much, our parents spoke for us. They promised that, when we came of age, we would be wed. That I would rule next to you, and we would join our households to make it so our reign would be that of legends. We would usher in a new life for the Amari, one above ground. Where the humans would be the ones fearing us, not the other way around."

He circled her. "Can't you see them, Serafina? The throngs of people around us, bending their knee? All wearing their best clothes, there to watch the promise of a better life unfold before them. They're waiting for us. They want us to finish the ceremony, pledge to bring them out of hiding and turn on those who have enslaved us."

Fin whimpered in pain as his hands dug into her shoulders, forcing her to sit upright. "I don't remember that, James. I saw it, but I was in the crowd. I'm not the person you think I am. Please, just let me go." Her voice cracked.

Hands grabbed her chin, forcing her head up. James knelt in front of her. "Just say the words, that's all you have to do. No one needs to know if you're real or not. They just want a figurehead. I can't be that, but you can. You're the key to everything I've wanted in life. So, do what you're told and I'll take most of the chains away. Not all, though. You're chained to me for the rest of your life. Get used to it."

She knew she was crying, but didn't care. The one thing she couldn't do was lie. Or live a life based on one.

She didn't remember moving her head, denying him what he wanted. What she felt was the crushing weight as her body was bombarded by chains from every direction. She slid to the floor, desperate for the connection to the earth that was fading from her soul.

Chapter Eleven

"**B**itch! How dare you defy me!"

The scream echoed through the twisting passageway. Alaric's stomach lurched at the sound of James' voice. He charged toward the sound, praying they would arrive before Fin's captor became even more enraged.

The tunnel opened up, revealing the abandoned city. He didn't care about his surroundings. The circle of light drew him forward. That's where James was holding her. He knew it.

"Trystian, you and Gwen watch Alaric's back. Make sure he can get to Fin. Don't get in my way unless I fall." There was a calmness in Emile's voice that scared Alaric. Something big was about to go down, bigger than rescuing Fin. He'd seen Emile track someone before, but not with this much drive. For a brief moment, he almost felt sorry for James. What Emile would do to him was not going to be pretty.

"I'll distract him, Emile. It's long past time. For both of us." Lyssa nodded, her gold eyes bright in the limited light.

Alaric watched, amazed, as Emile's eyes turned to the same metallic gold. He was Amari? "Of course. I took this task up over twenty years ago. It's been a long time coming." Giving Alaric a crooked smile, he nodded once. "Remember the promise you made, my friend. She's the only one that matters." Silently, the small man slipped off into the shadows.

A slap across his chest brought Alaric's attention forward again. Gwen gave him a serious look. He hooked his bow across his chest. It wasn't needed. Not here.

He could see James now. The man stood at the center of the courtyard, staring down at a pile of chains. Alaric's heart shattered as James shifted and he saw Fin's red hair jutting out from some of the links. *Please, Fin. Be alive. You called...I came!* He sent the thought, filled with desperation and love, toward the prone figure.

"She can't tell you a lie, James. Even you know that. The chains can compel her to do many things, but not that." Lyssa's voice rang out.

She stood at one section of the arc, hands folded, waiting for James to react to her.

He turned, sneering. "What do you know of these things? You hid! While she ran for her life, you hid from your own family and pretended to be one of *them*!"

Lyssa stood her ground. "I did what I was told, James. I always did. The goal was for me to stay alive, not be a pawn for those who would enslave the last member of the Amari royal family. But you knew that. You remember the day I stood in this square. And how you stood behind your brother as he and I were sealed to rule together." She sighed. "Or did your memory wipe out that part? It was never you, James. There was no betrothal. Only an agreement to rule jointly between our families. It was your jealousy, your disgrace, that led to the raid."

Alaric watched as James started to walk toward Lyssa. As soon as he was far enough away, he sprinted for Fin's prone form.

"It wasn't like that! They promised us sanctuary! Said that we'd be able to live out in the open, not in some hole in the ground!" James insisted.

Gwen knelt next to him, helping him lift the chains off of Fin's body. Alaric shoved at the links covering her head. Her eyes fluttered slightly. Leaning over, he kissed her cheek gently. "It's me, Fin. Alaric. If you call."

Pain and love reflected in her eyes as she smiled softly. "You will come." A sigh escaped her lips as her eyes closed.

"No…no…no! Fin! Stay with me!" Alaric could hear fighting behind him. Gwen was gone, leaving him alone to save her. He had to get the chains off of Fin.

The loose metal wasn't the hard part. Ten separate bands encircled her arms. Her dress lay halfway up one leg, revealing even more. Her chest barely moved. He didn't have time to waste.

Cursing, he began to unlatch each band of iron as he found it. The skin underneath, all red and blistered, made her convulse as the cool cavern air hit it. But her breathing gradually got stronger.

It felt like an eternity, but he finally got to the final band. Fitted around her left ankle, Alaric cursed. There wasn't a latch to be found. It was an owner's band.

"Fin, come on. You have to wake up. Please, wake up." Alaric turned his attention to rousing her. Glancing over his shoulder, he saw death. Gwen was on the ground, a pool of blood staining the stone under her. Trystian was on his knees, retching blood, as James stood over him. Lyssa was at the edge of the battle, being held back by Christoph.

And then Emile was there, behind James. A flash of silver across his neck, and James crumpled to the ground. Alaric shifted focus to Fin's ankle, grabbing at the final band as it popped loose. He put all his strength into throwing it as far away from Fin as he could.

"Alaric?"

Fin's voice, weak but steady, grabbed his attention. "I'm here. It's over now." He smoothed some hair away from her face. "You're free."

He helped her sit up, cradling her in his arms where she wouldn't see the price her friends had paid.

73 • Amari: Three Tales of Love and Triumph

Chapter Twelve

Fin watched the storm clouds gathering. Rain was coming, and fast. She smiled. Emile used to love the rain. Said it would make it harder for anyone to find them.

He was buried when they returned. Gwen was as well. Trystian recovered, and moved on. He seemed intent on starting over. Fin could understand why.

The full story would never be understood. She knew that. The Amari knew the raid was being planned, and took precautions. Emile swore to keep her safe, and the rumor of her being royal alive at the same time. So that Lyssa could be safe. In the end, it had cost him his own life. Too many years of using steel and his own magic to keep Fin alive.

Fin understood, to some degree. Her hand caressed her swollen abdomen, eager to meet the child growing within her. Ever since she and Alaric learned she was pregnant, she understood even more. Emile may not have been family, but she saw him as a father protecting his daughter.

A single knock at the door echoed through their small home. Smiling, she rose and answered it.

Alaric stood in the rain. "If you call," he said.

She took his hands into hers. "You will come," she whispered, pulling him into her arms.

***

Christoph leaned back in his chair, pushing his empty plate away. "Not sure I should say this," he hesitated, "but I think Alaric's a better cook than the ones in the palace."

"Only from necessity. Trystian was the real chef among us." Alaric stood, picked up his plate, and moved to the small counter that served as their kitchen area. "Christoph, how about some air?" he asked.

The other man looked at him, confusion on his face. Alaric pointed over to their wives, deep in conversation.

"Oh, ah, yeah," the man sputtered. "Sounds good to me."

The pair left quietly. Alaric knew Fin was close to the end of her pregnancy. She hardly left their home now, complaining about how lonely things could be. Having Lyssa and Christoph come over to eat was his idea. Fin was so used to people around her, she didn't take solitude well.

The two men settled into a pair of chairs that sat underneath a small overhang. "She's giving Lyssa ideas, you know."

"Those two get enough ideas between them to change the world. Putting them together may have been a mistake," Alaric laughed.

"She wants us to have a child. Started talking about how secure things are now, that my line needs to continue." Christoph leaned back in his chair, running a hand through his hair. "I just don't know that I'm ready for fatherhood."

"No one's ever ready for it, Christoph," Alaric replied. "You do have a bit more pressure on you than I ever did though."

"I know," he sighed. "One day I'm glad I'm the king, the next…"

"You want to run away from it." Alaric finished for him. "I know that feeling. Far too well." For a moment, he let his mind drift back to his childhood back on the island. It wasn't perfect, but it was good. There were times, when his brother was sick, he prayed for him to recover. If only to spare Alaric from inheriting the throne.

"You know, Fin told me something about you when you were gone. Wouldn't mind getting the story from you, though."

Alaric turned, his brow furrowed. "Just what did she tell you?"

"When I told her you were heading back to Lorien, she asked if Kaerdan was still on the throne. Though she didn't use those words."

"Exactly what words did she use?"

Christoph looked away, watching the few people wandering the street. "She called him 'not even half the man his brother is. And a rotten bastard that needed to be slit open'."

Alaric laughed, but there was no mirth in the sound. "That sounds like him. And her."

"Well?"

"Well, what?"

"Am I going to get the full story?"

Alaric looked down the street, choosing his words carefully. Christoph had been nothing but kind since they came here. No reason not to trust the man. But his own experiences with royalty made him leery. "It's a long one."

An elderly woman, flanked on each side by a youth, stopped in front of them. She bowed once, with great care, at Christoph.

The king rose, holding out his hands to greet the woman. "Great Mother, you honor me tonight. Will you now let me release you from your bondage?"

Alaric looked closer. A small iron bracelet encircled the old Amari woman's wrist. *Strange*, he thought, *Christoph set all the Amari free when he came to the throne. Why is she still wearing that?* It was the first time he'd seen any Amari in Caerlynn wearing any iron.

She nodded, "The time is come for the truth to be said. For all stories to be told." She leveled her gaze on Alaric. "Fin must learn the truth before her child comes. Before the first truly free Amari comes into this world. One whose parents never knew the burden of being a pet." She dug a withered hand into a satchel that hung across her body. Withdrawing a worn leather book, she looked back at Christoph. "I accept now, the freedom you have offered. And then I will discharge my most sacred task and give this to Seraphina nan Grear."

Christoph's hands moved to the woman's wrist. "And I am grateful, Great Mother, that I am honored to be the one to free you at last." He slid the bracelet across her bony hand, pocketing it as soon as it left her body. Standing aside, he watched as the old woman entered the house.

"Who was that?" Alaric asked, confused. "I've never seen her in town before."

Christoph settled back into his chair. "She was ancient when the raid happened on Uamh nan Amari. Stayed with Lyssa, raised her. Every other Amari my father chained deferred to her. I've tried, every year since he died, to get her to let me release her. She always said it wouldn't happen until her most sacred task was near completion. I never asked what that was. It felt…wrong for me to do so."

Alaric rose and started to move toward the door. Christoph stretched out an arm, blocking his way. "I wouldn't, my friend. Whatever is going on in there is for Fin and Fin alone. I know that much. I know you'll be told, in time. There are no secrets between the two of you. For now, though, I think we'll be out here for a while longer."

Settling back into his chair, Alaric kept a wary eye on the door. "I suppose so. But what do you propose we do while they're in there?"

The king smiled. "You did say the story was a long one. Looks like we've got the time."

Nodding, Alaric replied, "Yes, I think you're right."

Book Two:
Alaric's Bow

For the Archers of

The Barony of Glymm Mere.

May their aim ever be true.

Chapter One

Kai crouched behind the ferns and rocks, waiting. He'd been there since dawn. His legs no longer ached. They waited, like the rest of him.

At last, his patience rewarded him. A small rustle moved across the forest floor, carried on the breeze blowing toward him. The boar came into view. Kai's hand deftly notched the arrow he'd held loosely against the bow. Drawing back, he took aim. Today, he would be the one bringing home the prize for the feast. Not his brother.

The arrow flew through the air, plunging into the boar's side. It toppled over, dead. Kai stood, slinging his bow over his shoulder. He placed one hand on the rock in front of him, preparing to climb over it toward his kill. The clapping behind him halted his movement.

"Well shot, little one!" A deep voice dripped with sarcasm. "You managed to make it so we can go celebrate instead of staying out here for hours."

Kai turned. His older brother stood there, surrounded by his cronies. "I killed it, Kaerdan. That's not yours."

Kaerdan stepped forward. "It doesn't matter, does it? Because they'll all say it was mine." With one hand, he gestured at his cronies swarming the dead animal. Ruffling Kai's brown hair as he walked past him, he laughed. "Grow up, brother. There's nothing you can do to prove otherwise. You're the spare. I'm the heir. You're just a backup in case something happened to me as a child. Father never intended for you to take the throne. He never has. He couldn't even give you a proper name."

"Our mother named me, same as you," Kai called after his brother. All Kaerdan did to acknowledge his words was a rude gesture as he went to see "his" trophy.

Sighing resolutely, Kai took his time to gather his pack and make the walk back to the keep. He should've known better. All his life, his brother had taken credit for things Kai had done. Laid claim to things he liked. Reminded him, at every chance, that he was the lesser son.

Their parents didn't fight for him whenever he pressed his case. Respect your brother, for he will be King after your father. He will marry well—unite the residents of the island. Once that happened, they would be a force to be reckoned with. As long as the factions warred with each other, they couldn't regain what had been lost.

There wasn't much room for him once Kaerdan's marriage took place. Sure, Father would rule a few more years. Barring some accident or early death, that is. The earliest he would abdicate in favor of Kaerdan would be after he produced his own heir. And that was never certain.

He'd heard the stories from his mother. Of a land rich with resources. Farms and forests, cities and ports. His grandfather's court, where ladies wore beautiful jewels and men wore cloaks woven of pure silver. Where even the Amari wore chains studded with emeralds and rubies.

His mother filled his head with tales during his youth. She never said it, but he knew she missed the trappings of her father's palace. The bitterness that tinged her voice when she spoke of coming to the island and marrying her father wasn't well masked. Over time, she even stopped hiding it.

"If I could, I'd send you there, Kai. You'd be able to marry far more advantageously than you would here. What's left, after Kaerdan weds? That old fool that calls himself King to the North, Ian. He didn't have enough sense to father a son. No, just a daughter. And only one! How can you be expected to marry someone equal to us in station? There's barely any pure bloodlines left on this backward island!" Her contempt rang in his ears at the memory.

***

The bright sun reflected off the high stone walls of the main keep. Kai squinted against the glare as he emerged from the sheltering woods. He could see Kaerdan and his friends, shouting about how "great" the hunt was, crossing the far field. The Amari working the crops paused to give respect, but said nothing. It didn't surprise him. Many feared what would become of them when Father died. Almost as much as Kai wondered himself.

It didn't really matter, in the end. He knew he'd be leaving the island once Kaerdan wore the crown. His brother had made it very clear that he saw Kai as little more than an inconvenient brother. Five years separated them. It might as well be fifteen for how big the gulf between them was.

He heard the tall grain to the left of the path rustle, knew the lightness of the step as Holly drew up beside him. Amari or not, she was a friend. One of the few people he'd miss when he left.

"I see the Prince has decided what is his is yours once again," she said.

Kai shrugged. "It doesn't matter. Let him have the glory. I'd rather choke on rotten meat than eat at table with him."

She laughed. "If it matters so little, why does it eat at you so much? At least you still have your freedom. You can come and go as you desire. You're of age now. Take your leave of your father and find your own way."

He stopped and turned to look at her. Resisting the urge to tuck a stray lock of brown hair back under her bonnet, he smiled at her. "And who would take care of you if I did? Maybe I should go to Father tonight, let him know

I want you as my own." His grin faded as he saw the muscles in her face tense up.

"If that is your will, Prince." The title came out of her like a hiss. "What is it to be Amari but to serve those who chain us?"

Reaching out a hand, he hesitated as he saw her draw back. "That's not what I meant and you know it. Amari or not, I'd take you with me as a friend. Nothing more. Not unless you asked."

Holly looked at him, the gold eyes aflame with anger and fear. "That's the problem, Prince. You are not the one who is chained and must obey." She bobbed a quick curtsey, "By your leave. I have duties I must attend to." Without another word, she dove back into the wheat field.

Kai's mood was still black as he entered the keep. Much as he liked Holly, he didn't understand her most days. The Amari here weren't treated badly. They had shelter; homes were kept warm and dry from the winter snows. They had work to keep them busy, clothing and shoes given to them. None went hungry. And it's not like Father demanded them to use magic often. Sure, it happened sometimes. But the wars were long over. Few bore the scars of what they'd been commanded to do. For the last sixteen years, there'd been peace. The pact joining a seven-year old Kaerdan to the newborn, Jenny, when she reached eighteen was enough to keep things quiet.

He crossed the courtyard, not seeing the bustle about him. He just couldn't understand what Holly's problem was. It's not like he'd be a bad master to her. And it really was time for him to start establishing his own household. Second son or not, he was still a Prince. One that could travel with an entourage, have his own Amari. And one as gifted as Holly was would be an asset when he was looking for a bride.

A loud grumble from his stomach reminded him he'd left before breakfast. Rather than disturb anyone, he took a left at the next junction and headed down to the kitchens. Olive would be there, and she always had food for him.

The kitchens were a flurry of activity. Dozens of Amari darted about, intent on their duties. Few paid much attention to him as he entered, too focused on the tasks at hand. Kai stopped short before he collided with a pair of men hauling the boar he killed less than an hour earlier on a spit between them. He watched, curious, as they situated the iron rod on the notches above the huge cooking fire.

"Is someone coming?" he remarked to the room at large.

"Aye, Prince. Your brother's bride and her family sent word. The roads are good and they'll be here by the evening meal." Olive spoke, not looking up from the huge pile of dough she was kneading on the table in front of her. "We'll be celebrating a wedding in the morning."

Kai stepped back slightly, dodging another person as they hurried past with a bowl of fruit. "Tomorrow? Is it that soon?"

"Helen, get that bread in the oven right away!" Olive called out instructions better than a military commander. "Indeed it is. We thought we'd have another week or more to prepare. Watch the broth, Tobias! Burn that and you'll eat naught else for a week!"

Slowly, Kai retreated from the kitchen, grabbing a small meat pie from an unguarded bowl as he left. Had he remained, he would've been one more person in the way.

As he twisted his way through the stone corridors, he found himself dodging more and more people as they hurried about. Bunches of fragrant lavender and sage dotted the walls, chasing away the lingering mustiness of the castle. Clouds of dust could be seen rising in the air as tapestries were beaten clean. All to make a good first impression on the woman who would sit next to Kaerdan on the throne.

No longer caring, Kai retreated to the solitude of his chamber.

Chapter Two

Kai stuck to the shadows, avoiding the revelry of the wedding feast. A sense of dread had encompassed him since the arrival of the bridal party the day before. Something was wrong, but he couldn't put his finger on what.

Kaerdan and his new wife, Jenny, sat at the head table, their fathers flanking the happy couple. Her blonde hair shone in the candles illuminating the hall. Kaerdan did have a preference for fair-haired ladies. In that, he would be happy.

It was his mother, however, that drew his attention. She rarely left her rooms any more, claiming illness. Tonight, though, no sign of sickness decorated her pale face. If anything, it glowed in triumph. And why shouldn't it? Her firstborn married, ready to continue the family name. Soon, he would be King.

His father rose from his place, chalice in hand. "Today was a glorious day! A wedding, a new treaty, and a successful hunt! Kaerdan is truly gifted and his prize sits radiant beside him. To the happy couple!"

Kai shifted through the people near him. Gifted, indeed. The only thing his brother had ever been able to do was take credit for someone else's deeds.

He needed air. The hall was nauseatingly sweet, between the overabundance of the beeswax candles to the boar—his kill—roasting on the spit. Winding his way through the drunk wedding guests, he made his way to the upper gallery. Outside would've been preferable, but he knew better. At some point, he'd be expected to go forward and pledge his loyalty to his father and brother. Not that the words meant anything to him. He stopped believing in the vow after seeing how little they meant to Kaerdan.

"Where's the Historian?" his father's voice boomed through the arched hallway. Kai smiled a little. The recitation of the family line would take a good deal of time. Tradition, yes. But it also gave him enough time to breathe some air not saturated with sweat, ale, and food.

"Kai," Holly whispered from a recessed doorway. "Do you trust me?"

He blinked at her, puzzled. "Of course. Why wouldn't I? It's not like you can lie to me." He flinched at the anger that flashed across her face. She didn't need the reminder of her status.

"You need to come with me. Now." Reaching out, she pulled at his hand. Her voice tumbled over the words.

In the back of his mind, he heard the Historian drone on. He was covering the family fast. The old Amari had been with them since he was an infant, and was tasked with remembering each birth and death. Every family on the island kept a Historian to prove noble birth.

"Holly, I can't. As soon as Old Josiah is done, I have to go down and make my pledge. If I miss that, Father will have my hide."

She licked her lips, her gold eyes darting past him. "Kai, there won't be any way around that. Once Josiah is finished, things are going to go bad for you. Quickly." She pulled on his hand once again. "Please, I beg you. Come with me now while you can still run." Her eyes welled up with tears.

"Run? What am I running from?"

The hall below became silent. Too silent. He heard his father's massive oak chair slide across the floor. "Josiah, you forgot one of my sons. Why did you not add Kai to the list?"

Tearing his arm from Holly's grasp, Kai turned and looked down. Something knotted in his stomach. Whether it was fear or apprehension, he didn't know.

"I am Amari," the old man croaked. "I cannot lie. You asked for a recitation of the legitimate line. I have given you that."

Susana, his mother, spoke across the chamber. Her voice snapped with irritation and fear. "No, Josiah. Kai is true born. He should be on your list."

"Prince Kai is son of his Majesty, yes. But not by you, my Queen. He was begotten on an Amari brought over after a raid. You traded your own stillborn son to his mother so he might live. His only saving grace being his eyes were that of his father, not his mother. Kai is half Islander, half Amari."

The assembled guests broke out in a fury of voices. Kai staggered back against the wall, stunned. He was half Amari? Kaerdan'd have him in chains the moment he saw him.

Something pulled at his wrist, hard, insistent. He looked, afraid it was a guard. Already he could hear his brother demanding both Kai's attendance and a blacksmith. Holly stood next to him, her face full of compassion. "Kai, please. We have to get you away from here, now. Before it's too late!"

Fear released him from his shock. Nodding, he followed her as she led him through a back staircase. The dust, thick on the walls, gave him a small sliver of hope they'd make it out. The few that came through here were servants. Kaerdan probably didn't know it even existed.

"We knew, the moment the message came about their arrival, that it would come out tonight. Plans were made. We can get you off the island. But, please, you have to promise never to come back." Holly's whispered voice kept him focused.

Kai moved quickly, keeping pace with his friend. "Who is 'we'?"

Holly looked back at him as she halted in front of a small door. "There's a small rowboat just down the path.

We put your bow, some food, and a pouch of gold inside. Head to the docks, find Captain Ellory. He's expecting you as passenger. You'll sail as soon as you're on board."

Kai stopped her from darting off. "Who is this 'we' you keep talking of? Please, I need to know."

Her golden eyes no longer held back the tears. "Olive. She's our mother. Your true mother."

He knew what was going to happen to them once it came out they helped him escape. "Holly, come with me. I know what Kaerdan's going to do to the two of you."

"I can't." She lifted the hem of her skirt, displaying the iron band circling her ankle. Embracing him, she whispered, "Go, my brother. One of our family needs to remain unchained." .

He put his hand to the lever, ready to raise it. "Holly, what's my name? I don't know any more."

She whispered in his ear, and then pushed him out the door.

Kai ran down the path, his ears straining to hear any pursuers. As promised, the small skiff waited for him. He pushed off, rowing with strong strokes. Escape mattered more than anything right now.

The docks were a short distance away, and he was running short on time. By now, the castle had been searched and Kaerdan would be sending out parties to find him.

A lone figure stood on the closest pier, a massive merchant ship bobbing gently in the waves behind him. Three men appeared near the sandy beach, grabbing the bow and pulling him ashore. Kai grabbed at his bow and pack as he climbed out. The man he first saw approached.

"You the passenger I was told to expect?"

"Depends. Are you Captain Ellory?" The two men fell into step together, quickly moving across the dock and onto the ship.

"Aye, that I am. I understand there's a bit of a hurry to things. But can an old Captain know the name of his passenger?"

"The name's Alaric."

Chapter Three

The crossing would take over a week, which suited Alaric fine. He needed time to himself to decide what to do next.

Changing his name had been easy. Too easy. Ever since Holly whispered it in his ear, it felt right. More like who he was than Kai had ever been.

That first night, he'd mourned. Said good-bye to a mother and sister he'd never really known, who were most likely dead by now. If not dead, then they prayed for it swiftly. Kaerdan would punish them first. It was his way.

As to his other family, he scarcely thought on them. The feeling he'd had his entire life of being on the outside looking in made sense now. He didn't wholly belong there.

Nor was he fully Amari.

The second day was harder. Alaric stared at the polished brass mirror in his cabin for an hour, trying to see if there was any of the telltale gold coloring in his eyes. He'd heard of this, yes. Half-bred Amari were common enough, but almost all had the eye color. He would be one of the very few who could pass as human.

While that would make things easier, he also knew what he couldn't do. Going to his grandfather's palace was out of the question. Even if a messenger didn't make it before he did, it wouldn't be far behind. No, Kai had to die. Disappear. Never to be seen or heard from again.

The crew left him alone, which suited him just fine. How Holly procured his passage he'd never know. He needed the time and solitude right now.

A light knock at the door to his small cabin roused him from his thoughts. He turned his head around as the door swung open, the wood creaking slightly. Captain Ellory slipped into the room, closing the door behind him.

"Pardon the intrusion, but something's happened you need to know about."

Alaric nodded, gesturing for the Captain to sit in the only chair in the room. He settled on his bunk, waiting.

Ellory sank into the chair. Alaric noticed both relief and concern on the man's weather-beaten face. Whether or not the man's gray hair was from age or worry he couldn't tell. Outside of being older, there was no way to determine the Captain's age. Though, at eighteen, there many people who fit that statement.

"I know who you are, what you are. Holly and I go way back. I was the one who brought your mother, your real mother, to the Island. I've regretted every single trip your father took that ended with a chained Amari in the hold. Helping you escape isn't much, but it makes me feel better. The trick will be putting you ashore without anyone being the wiser."

Alaric nodded. "I know where not to go, but that's about it. I've never had to reinvent my life before." He ran a hand through his brown hair. "I'm fair with a bow. Maybe I could make my way to another King's holding, hide there as a hunter for his table."

Ellory shook his head. "Bad idea. Your brother won't stop until he's found you, made an example. You're a direct challenge to his rule. He'd like nothing more than to see you kneeling at his feet, a chain around your neck."

Shrugging, he replied, "He can have the entire island for all I care. I won't be going back there any time soon."

"Won't matter. Not to the likes of him. For all his bluster, he's an insecure brat. He knows you're a better man than he'll ever be. Until he can break you, he won't stop."

Pausing, the older man picked at a callous on the palm of his hand. "I've got another passenger. About your height, coloring. He died in the night." He held a hand up to stop Alaric's shocked words before they were spoken. "No, we didn't do anything to him. He was sick before he came on board. When we get to Lorien, we're going to swear that the passenger that died was a man we were hired to pick up in the dead of night. Near Caer Mikkel. The news will be reported to your Grandfather, who will send the message to your father and brother. And you can live your life."

Stunned, he absorbed the news. The Captain was handing him the chance to live without looking over his shoulder. "I don't know what to say..." he looked at the other man.

Ellory rose, holding out his hand in parting. Alaric grasped it in return. The captain slapped his shoulder with his free hand. "Go. Use that bow of yours, yes, but don't stay in one place too long. Rent it out for private wars, mercenary work. You're alive, and we've made the best we can to cover your trail. Now you have to keep low enough to stay alive."

As the captain turned to leave, Alaric voiced the question he'd had on his mind for days. "Captain, why help me like this? What did Holly give you?"

A tired smile crossed the man's face. "Like I said, I owed a debt. Those of us who can hide tend to help those who need it."

Alaric's eyes grew wide as the pale blue of the captain's eyes fell away, briefly replaced by the telltale gold. Without another word, he watched the man walk out the door.

***

Two days later, he awoke to the sound of shouted orders and a flurry of footsteps on the deck above. Alaric pulled on his breeches as he stared out the small porthole. They'd arrived at Lorien.

He dressed quickly, choosing a green tunic. Holly had only packed three outfits, none of them anything that would proclaim his former rank. Maybe someday he'd be able to buy her freedom. But that would mean confronting Kaerdan.

"Put it from your mind, lad." Ellory's voice called out from the doorway. "You're not going to be able to save her. Her fate was sealed the moment she concocted your escape."

"You don't know that. Kaerdan might—" he started to say, shoving the last few belongings into his pack.

"No, he won't. You and I both know she's either dead, or wishing she was. And she knew it when she made her choice. Amari can't take any risks without repercussions, even those of us who are free. The magic we harness won't let us. There's always a price to be paid for our actions."

Alaric strapped his quiver to the side of his pack. "I can't accept that."

"Doesn't change it. If you want to repay her, then do what you can to save any Amari you run across. If you end up in an army, offer to watch over them. Show them kindness instead of brutality. And, if you ever find one who's stayed hidden and unchained, make sure they stay that way. Holly didn't give up her life so you could take her place in chains. She did it so her brother could save others."

Alaric looked away, slipping his pack onto his back. Ellory's words hit home. He was right. Holly was either dead, or wished she were. Kaerdan wouldn't have been kind to her. Or Olive. The only one who might have been spared his wrath was his mother. His hand molded around the center of his bow through the covering. If nothing else in his life made sense, that still did.

"You may not have the eyes, Alaric. Be grateful for that. But you've got some sort of magic going on between you and that bow of yours. Just make sure the rest of the world thinks it's skill and nothing more. You might want to miss every now and then."

Pausing at the door, he held out his hand to the captain. "Thank you. For everything."

Ellory shook his hand. "You've got a debt to pay, lad. And you can't do that if you're in chains. Remember that."

Alaric nodded in understanding. Without another word, he wound his way up to the deck and then down to the dock.

He paid close attention to where he was going, dodging between stacks of crates, sailors, and laborers. The wooden platform below him swayed with movement from above. The violent motion would've tripped him if it wasn't for the week at sea.

Stepping off the dock and onto the dirt road, he moved to one side. Partly to stay out of anyone's way, and so he could take a good look around him.

The city was laid out in a series of terraces cut into the hillside. The level people resided on depended on their rank. Situated at the top, looking down on everything, was his grandfather's palace. The white walls shimmered in the early morning sun. With a sigh, he realized it wasn't his grandfather that lived there. His welcome would be deceptively warm…right up until they chained him and put him on the first boat back to face Kaerdan.

He reached behind him and pulled the hood of his mantle over his head. There was no way of knowing if word had reached Lorien yet, but it wouldn't suit him to be reckless. He had to find a job, one that took him out of the city.

Alaric spent another few minutes studying the throng of people around him. Watching who moved where, who carried what.

"Pardon, sir, are you hungry?" a small voice piped up.

Looking down, he saw a young girl with a tray full of meat pies staring at him. Her gold eyes stood out on her dirty face. His stomach grumbled loudly. Laughing, he replied, "Well, there's your answer. How much for a pie?"

"They're a half crown, if you please. We just made them fresh this morning."

Reaching into his tunic, he pulled a coin out from a hidden pocket. Handing it to the child, he tried not to stare at the scars on her forearm. "There you are, one half crown. Do I get my pick?"

The girl quickly pocketed the money and held the tray a bit higher. "Yes, sir. Whichever one you'd like."

He barely had the pastry in his hand before she scampered off to another person. Poor child had been forced to use her magic already, and in ways that caused harm. Holly had taught him how it worked. How the magic rebounded on the Amari, scarring them in some way for the harm caused. His father had known about it, and never made them cause harm unless it was in self-defense. Whoever this child belonged to had no such morals.

He began to meander down the street, munching on the pastry as he walked. If he could find a central market of some kind, join up with a caravan as a guard that would take him out of town.

After a few minutes, he knew enough of the area to realize he had to move inward. Closer to the city gates leading inland. The only people hiring near the docks wanted sailors. While he hadn't been sick on the crossing, he knew he wasn't cut out for that kind of life.

Two streets over, he heard the auctioneer's voice carry over the crowd around him. One last lot for the day. An Amari family. His chest tightened as he forced himself towards the market. A caravan heading inland would be perfect for him to hide in. And, if his luck held, he'd be able to help a few people along the way.

The crowd thinned out as he approached the small courtyard where the auction was being held. A few still stood in front of the wooden platform, absently raising a hand in answer to the auctioneer's bidding. A few others milled about a table, exchanging coin and signing parchment. Over to the left, against a stone building, a third man read over the parchments handed him and completed the transfer of ownership. The whole thing, while done quietly and openly, turned Alaric's stomach.

The auctioneer called out, "Sold!" a final time, signaling the end of the day. Alaric watched the family of three being led off the platform. Another man stood not far from the bookkeeper's table. Alaric watched as he moved forward to pay. He was strong, sure. His beard hid most of his face. The robes he wore were long, nothing like anything Alaric had seen before. Vibrant colors in strange patterns. Wherever he was from, it wasn't close.

He continued to watch the robed man, waited until he finished the transfer and began to lead the family away from the market.

"Pardon, sir," Alaric stepped in front of the group. "I'm looking for work."

The man's brow furrowed slightly. "What kind of work?"

Shrugging, he responded. "About any I can find. Got a bit of a nagging need to see another part of the world."

"You any good with that thing?" The man pointed at the bow sticking up from the pack.

Alaric glanced back, noticed the covering had slipped loose. Looking forward again, he said, "Good enough to help feed you and your men on the way home."

"We'll see. Earn your keep and you'll be paid when we arrive. Don't, and I'll leave you at the first hovel I care to."

"Fair enough. Where are we headed?

"Antioch. Hope you got good shoes, boy. You'll be walking in them for the next four months."

Chapter Four

Alaric woke, the morning sun blazing through the small window of his room. Three years in Antioch and he still wasn't used to the heat.

Rising, he poured some water from the ewer into the basin. Splashing the cool water over his face, he drew a deep breath. Every year, this day had been the hardest. The official visit from the Lorien contingent. He didn't go out of his way to draw notice to himself, never had. His skin had slowly darkened over the years, his brown hair lighter from the sun. The beard he now wore still itched, but he'd gotten used to it. Mostly.

Still, he kept his guard up. There was always the chance Kaerdan hadn't bought the lie that he died on the ship. His brother was nothing if not thorough. Until he saw a body, there was a chance Kai still lived.

Only no one here would know that name. To this city, he was Alaric. Still an Islander, yes. There was no way to hide that. But they'd accepted him, his story. At least, he hoped they had.

Knowing his absence along the procession route would be missed, he sighed. Erien wouldn't let him sit this one out. She'd asked so many questions when first they met about his home. In the beginning, he feared she was one of Kaerdan's spies. When the questions stopped and no one came, he relaxed a little. Erien had lived a life in this desert oasis is all. She dreamed of a land where water was plentiful. Though she scoffed at the idea of snow.

A light rapping at his door startled him. "Alaric, you up yet?" A female voice muffled by the thick wood.

"Yeah, hold on." He grabbed a caftan off of the peg on the wall. Tossing it over his head, he straightened out the folds as he walked toward the door.

Opening it, he was treated to a grin from his friend. "If I'd known you weren't dressed yet, I wouldn't have waited out here." Erien teased him.

"If I'd let you in while I was naked, your father would've had me drawn and quartered before the procession even started," he laughed in return. Closing the door behind him, he waited for her to move forward.

Her black hair, the long braid dangling down below her headscarf, swayed as she spoke. "Not if he knows what's good for him. The only hope he has for me to agree to any match he proposes for me is to not interfere with my friendships."

Alaric fell into step next to her, "Friendships? Is that the term they use around here?"

Erien laughed, "Not all the time, no. But Father and I worked out what I can and cannot do some time ago. He allows me the freedom to befriend those I want to, knowing nothing will become serious. And I accept a suitable candidate for my hand."

"The key word there being 'suitable', I suppose."

"Absolutely." She glanced back at him as they made their way down the narrow spiral staircase. "There's lots of men who would marry me simply because of who he is. I want someone who is more interested in who I am than his balance sheet."

"And some Islander doesn't count?"

She turned, craning her neck to meet his eyes. "Alaric, you know you have his trust and admiration. You earned that by finding food when no one else could on that first caravan trip. But his position would be in jeopardy if he let us be together in that way. You and I both know his true nature. The rest of Antioch thinks of him as a ruthless slave trader. Even the Amari he brings back learn how to speak of him without lying but not telling of his kindness toward them. As long as Ajanor rules, and is friendly with Lorien, he cannot let his true nature show."

Alaric nodded. Ajanor was brutal when it came to how he treated the Amari. More died under his command each year. The treaty with Lorien was ironclad and suited both kingdoms well. The smaller kingdoms feared them, and rightly so. The wars waged had slowly chipped away at borders. In just the last three years, Antioch had annexed two of its neighbors. One didn't even bother to fight.

Lorien wasn't far behind. Rumor ran before the official visit, like always. Kaerdan now ruled the island with an iron fist. An alliance between him and Lorien seemed imminent, allowing Lorien access to the fleet of ships at his brother's command. Adding Antioch's forces to the mix would make it possible for war to ravage almost every kingdom in the world. What scared him even more, though, was what would happen the day the alliance fell apart.

The bright sunlight exploded on them as Erien opened the door to the street outside. Alaric raised the hood of his caftan before stepping through the portal.

The avenue was already crowded with people eagerly awaiting the annual spectacle. The visit, long ago established as a reason to celebrate, drew hundreds from the neighboring towns as well as caravans from farther away. The massive desert had several oasis points, waystations for caravans that grew into thriving cities and towns. Coming to the capital, though, was reserved for only tradesmen. Except for when Lorien visited.

Had his room faced the street, Alaric would've been content to watch from above. Erien, however, loved being in the middle of it all. She fed off the energy of the crowd, enjoyed the spectacle. To her, the outfits worn by the visiting dignitaries were exotic. He could sympathize. It took him time to get used to wearing a caftan over breeches and a tunic.

They found a place and waited. It wasn't long before the trumpets blared, heralding the dignitaries. The parade wove slowly past the throngs lining the streets. Musicians led the way, followed by a group of spearmen in full armor. The glare of the sun off the metal almost blinding those who looked too long. Then came the ornate, gilded litters. Each one sat on the shoulders of eight Amari men, clad in shirt and breeches. Alaric could see beads of sweat trickle down their faces as the heavy garments compounded the heat.

The curtains of each were pulled back, allowing the throngs to see the visitors in all their glory. Courtiers and diplomats lounged, richly embroidered and bejeweled fabrics clashed with the simplicity of the garments of those in the crowd. The fourth litter caused Alaric to clench his jaw.

Holly was one of the bearers, her head shaved. The tunic she wore, cut so no one would mistake her for a man, showed red skin with crisscrossed pale scars. The sun had been merciless to her during the journey, and so had Kaerdan.

She kept her eyes down as she passed. There was his brother, relaxing on a bed of satin pillows and a chalice in his hand. Nothing had changed in his appearance. The same arrogance and hard set to the jaw remained. He refused to look outside at the people around him.

He felt Erien shift next to him, breaking his evaluation of Kaerdan. Her form retreated toward a doorway where her father stood, motioning to her.

Alaric slid between the crowd, trying to follow. By the time he reached her, she was alone. Her face held a look he'd never seen before. It wasn't quite fear or anger, but a bit of both.

She looked up and saw him. Holding a single hand up, she silenced him before he could say a word. "Not here, my friend. And not now. Go to work. I'll tell you before noon."

With that, he watched as she slipped away into the crowd.

He didn't see her again for two hours. He was in the back of the shop, working on some fletchings under the awning, when she sat next to him. Grabbing a small knife and a feather, she began to cut into the shaft.

They sat there in silence for a few moments. "I'm to be married. Soon. My husband," contempt dripped from her voice, "is among the diplomats and is eager to take me home with him."

Alaric's gut tightened. "I thought you were granted the right to refuse a suitor."

"I was, initially. But now Ajanor has stepped in. He wants this alliance, and Father dared not refuse him."

He swallowed, fearing her answer to his next question. "Who is it to be, then? Some minor bureaucrat?"

She sighed. "No. Someone who claims to be King of the Islanders. Seems his wife died giving birth to a daughter two years ago and he's done grieving. That same daughter is now betrothed to one of Ajanor's younger sons. I'm part of the deal to secure the treaty." Angrily, she swiped the blade across the shaft of the feather. "Bartered and sold like an Amari, only with marriage vows binding me over a steel band around my ankle."

Alaric didn't dare speak. It could only be Kaerdan. Fear for his friend overtook him. "So, run. Leave. If you don't want this Island King, don't wed him."

The knife flew from her hand, lodging in a barrel across from them. "I can't. You and I both know this. I'm bound to obey my father and my King. This is the price I pay for the life I live."

Unable to contain himself, Alaric turned to her. He grabbed one of her hands and held it close. "Erien, don't do this. You don't know him. You'll regret this faster than you can imagine."

She snorted, "Strange words from an Islander. I always thought you saw your kings as gods walking the land." She pulled her hand from his. "It doesn't matter. The announcement is being made tonight, at the feast. Father asks that you attend, as well. He thinks showing this King he has Islanders under his employ will increase his position."

Alaric's eyes widened briefly. "He wants me there? No. I can't." He rose, a hand flying to his brow. His head was pounding faster than his heart.

"Alaric, what's wrong? You've never denied an invitation like this before. It's obvious you know my husband-to-be. If there's something my father should know, that I should know, about him then say it."

"I can't, Erien. You and your father know enough. I left the Island, and my life there, with reason. If Kaerdan were to even suspect I was here—"

"Erien, leave us." Rahjin's voice called out from the doorway. "This is a matter for men. Your mother waits on you to start preparations for the feast."

Alaric didn't turn as Erien left to obey her father's command. He didn't dare.

"If there is a tale I must hear, tell it now, Islander. Otherwise, your presence is needed tonight as I celebrate the coming marriage. I have let you live among my family for long enough now that you should trust me. Give me reason to excuse you from the feast that I can abide by."

Defeated, Alaric slumped onto a bench. "What do you know, Rahjin? Or guessed?"

The older man sat opposite him. "I know the story you gave on the way here was full of half-truths. That you are an Islander there is no doubt. From the north? I do not think so. The cloak you had wasn't thick enough to hold back the cold they face. Your skill with a bow was almost too good. While many from your lands can hunt well, you rarely missed. Even when the other hunters came back claiming there was no beast to be found, you'd find something. My next trip, you refused to go back to Lorien. I asked around. Seems the same time you showed up the year earlier, there were rumors about the new King having a half-Amari brother. One they thought was dead. But no corpse was found."

Alaric nodded, "You're not a foolish man, Rahjin. Kaerdan would repay you handsomely for turning me over. He may even agree not to beat your daughter once they're married."

"You are family, Alaric. You reside in my home, work for me. I will hold your secret. And excuse you from the feasting. Though I recommend you find a way out of the city soon. You, and your bow, will be missed. But your brother will find out about you if you remain. Too many others will remark about an Islander in my employ if you stay. As to Erien," he paused, "make no mistake. If I hear he has mistreated her in any way, the next breath he draws will be his last. And she will rule the Island then, not him." Rahjin rose. "Go. Pack your gear and find a tavern. Hire yourself off as a personal guard to someone else leaving the city. More are leaving than coming in now. I wish you well, my friend." He held out his hand to Alaric.

Grasping it, Alaric nodded. "Thank you. Tell Erien, well, tell her to ask for a gift from Kaerdan. There's an Amari with his party, a woman by the name of Holly. She'll serve Erien well."

"Any message you want sent to her?"

He shook his head. "No. It'll only put both of them at risk. Better she thinks her brother is dead, and Erien not know at all, than otherwise." He paused. "Thank you, again. You've given me refuge when it was needed. I won't forget that."

"Repay my kindness by doing the same for another. You'd do well as a mercenary, Alaric. As long as the cause is a just one."

Alaric walked into the shop without another word. Rahjin was right. He had to disappear. No good-byes. For the second time in less than four years, he was running. Only this time, he had allies to cover his trail.

Darting up the stairs to his small room, his mind raced. What to pack, what to leave behind. It really wasn't a hard decision. He knew he had to leave, tonight if possible. The months on the road to reach Antioch taught him what was important to carry with him. He'd not collected much since he lived here, either.

The packing was swift. He made sure his tunic and breeches were closer to the top this time, along with a razor. He changed into his sturdy leather boots, then moved aside the small chest of drawers. In the wall behind it, he worked the tip of his dagger into a barely noticeable gap in the boards. Reaching into the space, he pulled out two pouches full of coin. The benefit of never buying more than one needed. He had money for the journey ahead.

He secured one pouch deep within the pack, under several layers of clothing. His repair kit slid into a pocket next to the strap meant for his quiver. Carefully, he secured the wrapping around his bow. He wasn't sure if Kaerdan would recognize the carving, but now was not a time to take chances.

One last look around the room that had been home for three years to make sure everything necessary was packed. Shouldering his burden, he walked out the door without looking back.

Chapter Five

The tavern was full, even in this part of Antioch. Revelers mixed with thieves and pickpockets, each offering toasts to the happy couple. And the alliance in general. War was coming, and with it the chance for more profit.

Alaric kept to himself in a corner. He'd been here for two days now. No one was hiring, not yet. Wait a few days, they said. We want to celebrate first. The longer he waited, the more nervous he became.

One way or another, he was leaving by dawn. Even if it meant buying a camel. The next big city was still a good three days to the south. A horse was faster, but that meant extra feed, water. The camel could do the distance.

The wedding procession had wound through the streets that evening. Alaric stayed in his corner, avoiding the spectacle. Ale was his friend tonight. Though the three pints he'd downed so far had done little to dull the pain he felt.

He wasn't so far gone he couldn't keep an eye on his things, though. Or not pick up on small changes in the tavern. He saw the urchin who stole coin out of one pocket while pretending to wipe up crumbs, and the barkeep adding water to the keg when he thought no one was looking. Most of the guests, though, were too busy celebrating.

Not all, though. A group of four sat at a table in the opposite corner. Two women, two men. Warriors, a probable thief, and someone he couldn't figure out. Important, though, the way the other three watched around her. The red braid hanging straight down her back stood out like a beacon. More than one man approached the table, hoping to find out who she was. Each time, they were rebuffed by the other three.

"Entire town reeks right now, I'm telling you. Wish that Islander would take his Amari and leave already. It's bad enough with the ones that live here. This stinkin' lot can't even teach them to bathe." Alaric heard the bitter words of the man the next table over. He sipped at his ale, listening.

"What'cha talkin' about, Charlie? The foreigners are cleaner than you've ever been." Laughter overtook the group.

"Those Amari, they've got a smell about them. Not everyone can tell, but I can. It has to do with the magic they do. Especially the ones that are unchained. People need to leash their pets, you know. Otherwise they might get 'lost'."

More laughter erupted from the group. "Doubt there's any free for the takin' in this place, Charlie. Ajanor's stricter than most on his pets. Don't you remember? When we crossed into his lands last year, the checkpoints we had to go through. The man's paranoid that some unchained Amari's going to murder him in his sleep."

Out of the corner of his eye, Alaric watched the man they called Charlie shrug. "No skin off my nose if he's paranoid. I'm just tired of the stench. Can even smell it in here, and there's not a single one to be seen."

Trumpets blared outside. Alaric stayed seated while most of the room filed outside to see why. He knew why. The ceremony was finally over. Erien and her new husband were being paraded through the streets. He knew himself well enough to stay seated. Otherwise, he might do something he knew he'd regret.

He absently stared at the inside of his mug, watching the ale swirl around the bottom. He hated living in the shadows, watching life happen around him. All because others thought he was worth saving. Right now, he felt like he was the last person who should be saved. But he had no way of saving anyone else.

Another person slid into the seat opposite of him. "I hear you're looking for a job."

Raising his head, Alaric studied the older man. He'd been with the others, across the room. His dark hair blended with the collar of the tunic he wore. It was the thief.

"I might be. What's the job?"

"Just get myself and my companions to the border of Dunegan. Only a week or two at most, depending on how fast we travel. We're not familiar with travel in the desert and need a guide." The man's dark gaze was piercing. Whoever he was, he would know when Alaric was lying.

"When do we leave?"

The other man placed a hand on the table, pushing himself up. "Now. We're not big on celebrations, and we'd like to be on our way."

Alaric stood as well, though swaying slightly. "Fair enough." Grabbing his pack and wrapped bow, he followed the other man through the doorway.

The rest of the group were mounted on three horses. A fourth animal was saddled and waiting. A pack mule, laden with supplies, was led by the other man. The man who hired him vaulted up behind the red-haired woman. Her covering hid most of her features, and she kept her head down. Alaric moved toward the waiting horse. "You hired the drunk?" The other woman snorted.

"Something tells me he's going to be fine when he's sober, Gwen. And that he needs to leave here more than we do. You can ask him questions over dinner if you want. But the decision's mine." The man looked over at Alaric. "I'm Emile. That's Gwen." He nodded to the woman on the other horse. "Trystian's going to bring up the back with the supplies. We'll follow you." Emile nodded, expecting Alaric to take point.

He maneuvered his horse closer to Emile's. "What's your name, miss?" he asked the woman riding in front.

Her head swiveled. A pair of green eyes set in a pale face met his gaze. There was no fear, only a tired resignation in them. "It's Fin," she replied softly.

"Questions can wait. You were hired to lead us to the border. Let's go." Emile's voice was direct, commanding.

Alaric nodded. Whoever this Fin was, the rest were determined to protect her. He got the sinking feeling he'd just signed on for something far more dangerous than he originally thought.

***

Alaric held up his hand, signaling the group to stop. "We rest here. It's going to be too dark to keep going within an hour. And too cold." He turned in his saddle. "There's no oasis we can reach for at least a day's ride. The rocks over there—" he pointed to his left "—we put the tent against them. They'll shield us from any storms in the night." He guided his horse toward the formation, hearing the others follow behind.

Four hours of silence had marked the journey so far. He was sober now, not that it mattered. He wasn't that far into his cups to begin with. He knew the way to Dunegan, and how to get there safely. This part of the desert was tricky. Even the raiders stayed away most of the time.

Alaric busied himself with making a way for them to tether the horses for the night while the others erected the tent on the sheltered side of the rocks. "Is it safe for a fire?" Emile asked.

He nodded his head. "Should be, if you keep it small. Raiders, if they come, will wait for us to be farther from the city."

"We still keep watch." Trystian's deep voice was barely over a whisper.

"I don't think that's what he was suggesting, Trystian." Alaric raised his head at the sound of the woman's voice. Calm, soothing. And tired. Whoever this Fin was, she wasn't immune to that.

Emile led the woman over to a chair, making her sit. Gwen handed her a water skin. A whispered command of "Rest now, we've got things covered" as she did so.

Alaric tore his gaze from her. "I recommend we keep the horses saddled, though. Just in case." He kept his focus on the animals, but watched as the others put the tent up quickly. One side was left open, the canvas stretched out to give some shelter to the horses.

The large, bearded man called Trystian had a fire started by the time Alaric finished tending to the horses. A small pot, suspended over the flames, showed promise of a good meal. It wouldn't be much, but it'd be hot and filling.

Alaric set up his bedroll for the night. Not so close to the others that there'd be cause for alarm, but still within the shelter of the tent. He already knew they didn't trust him yet. No reason to push it.

"How long do you think we'll be on the road, Islander?" Gwen didn't look at him as she spoke.

He shrugged. "Depends. If we don't encounter any trouble, no more than a week. If we get caught up in a storm, could be two."

"Do raiders come through often?"

"They're usually more active closer to whatever oasis they operate from. If we stay on the main road, take no shortcuts, they probably won't bother us. I don't care much for Ajanor's policies, but he did right by having the army patrol the main route. If we put a coin or two into the right hands as we move along, no one will bother us."

Emile spoke up. "No worries there. I've got coin for that. I'd rather bribe a few officials than be set on in the night."

"Raiders are the least of our worries at night," Trystian's deep voice carried in the still night air. Glancing at the man, Alaric saw him raise his dagger. A large scorpion writhed on the tip. The black and red striped body made him swallow hard.

"Those are the worst out here. Can kill a man with a single jab, but rarely come near humans. If we keep the fire going, they'll stay away." Alaric stated with conviction.

"Hope so. If they get to one of the horses, you're the one walking the next day." Trystian pointed with his dagger, emphasizing his words. "Food's ready." He flicked the blade in his hand, sending the dead scorpion off into the night.

Conversation was sparse over the meal. Emile set up a rotation, but didn't mention Alaric in it. Not surprising, really. He was the guide, that's it. That he needed to get out of Antioch as badly as they seemed to want to wasn't mentioned.

He settled into his bedroll, staring at the sky for a time. Thousands of stars shone down on him. His mind drifted to Erien. It was her wedding night. Was Kaerdan being gentle with her? By the gods, he hoped so.

"You trust him." Fin's whispered voice reached his ears.

"Yes." Emile replied. "So will you, in time. It won't be any different than when Gwen or Trystian came across our path."

"I'm not so sure. There's something different about him." Alaric heard the hesitation in her voice.

"You still trust me, don't you?"

"Of course. Just as I have since you found me."

"Well, then. You trust me. I trust him. He's got almost as much to fear as you do, Fin. He's no slaver."

She muttered something else he couldn't understand. Whatever it was, the conversation was over.

Shrugging it off, he closed his eyes. They provided him a way out of Antioch. Away from any chance of Kaerdan finding him. Whatever secrets they had would either come out in the journey ahead, or not at all. One final prayer in hopes that Erien's life would not be what he feared it would be, and he let sleep overtake his body.

"Wake up, slowly. We have company." The whispered command drove sleep from his mind. Blinking, he stared up at the stars. Still an hour or two before sunrise. The horses pranced nervously. A dark figure, his back against the rocks near him, nodded once. "They're coming, slowly, from the road. Don't know they've been seen. Only five of them. Trystian, Gwen, and I will deal with them. Stay here, watch over Fin." Emile turned to him, his face a deadly mask. "If any of them get through us, put her on a horse and go. We'll catch up. If she's taken while there's still breath in your body, Islander, you'll wish you'd never heard of us."

Alaric eased out of his blankets, reaching for his bow as he rose. He kept his back to the road as he unwrapped it from the casing and slid the string into place. He took a moment to watch as Emile slid into the tent to wake the others. The two warriors rose with a practiced stealthiness, strapping on a few bits of armor too cumbersome to sleep in. Emile blocked his view of Fin.

Trying to move naturally, he sauntered the few feet to the horses. He'd left his quiver strapped to the saddle. Given the tenor of Emile's instructions, he pulled out just a few arrows. If they had to run for it, he'd need most to discourage pursuit.

Without warning, Trystian came charging out of the darkness of the tent, screaming. Gwen followed, bellowing a war cry that would scare the very rocks. Alaric barely spotted Emile slipping around the edges of the outcropping.

Alaric moved toward the opening of the tent. He stabbed five arrows into the ground so he could easily grab them, and notched a sixth. Their attackers were in range, but the shadows were still too deep to recognize friend from foe.

He heard Fin moving up behind him. "Stay back. I don't want to shoot you by accident."

Her exhale was more of a hiss than anything. "I can defend myself, even if he doesn't think so!"

Alaric thrust out his arm, blocking her stride. "Doesn't matter. And I never said you couldn't. But I'd rather piss you off than Emile. Something tells me he's deadlier than you."

He took his eyes off the combat to look at her. The red hair glowed in the faint light, framing her narrow face. Her green eyes glared at him, ready for a fight. He swallowed. Perhaps she was the deadlier of the two.

He nodded once as she stepped back, eyes still blazing with anger. The light was enough now to determine the combatants. He raised the bow, slowly drawing the string back to his ear. Taking aim, he released the arrow at precisely the right time, piercing one of the raiders through the neck as he moved in behind Gwen.

Snatching an arrow from the ground in front of him, he drew back again and let it fly. This one caught the raider mid-thigh, distracting him enough for Trystian's sword to get through his defenses.

A heavy thud reverberated through the ground behind him, followed by Fin's startled gasp. He grabbed another arrow as he pivoted, letting it fly as soon as he saw the back of the raider. The man screamed, letting loose his hold on Fin. A sword slashed toward Alaric's midsection, barely missing his tunic. He dropped the bow and drew out a dagger. "Fin! Get on my horse. Now!" he ordered, dodging another attack.

He kicked the bow toward her. His attention went off his opponent for a moment as he watched her grab it as she ran past. A searing pain bit into his left shoulder as the sword found a mark. Without thought, he drove forward and plunged his dagger into the raider's chest. His foe dropped to the ground, dead. Alaric grabbed the remaining arrows and headed to the horses. His vision blurred. The world spun, and then darkness overtook him.

Chapter Six

He didn't remember much. A fever, perhaps? Nightmares that made him sweat? He only knew pain that wouldn't end. And a voice that talked him through the black abyss.

The first few times he heard it, he couldn't place it. It was a woman's voice. Holly? Erien? Whoever it was, they told him to fight. Not to give in.

The darkness was so comfortable, though. It surrounded him like a blanket, cocooning him in warmth and security. He didn't have any worries here. No pain, no fears. Kaerdan wouldn't find him, ever. And it tempted him with that promise.

But still that soft voice persuaded him, coaxed him to shed the bindings around him. It was that voice that peeled away the layers of darkness.

As they left, the pain returned. Searing through his muscles, making him scream. It burned throughout his blood, tearing through his organs with jagged teeth. The woman's voice remained steady as his back arched and the sweat streamed down his face. Hours went by before sleep offered him an escape from the delirium.

How long he slept, he didn't know. Emile's voice was the first one to pierce the recesses of his brain, though.

"You're sure he's going to be able to travel soon? We can't stay here much longer, Fin. Gwen and Trystian aren't going to be able to keep everything away."

A woman answered, the same voice that had coaxed him back from death. "I'm sure. His wound's healed. If he was going to succumb to the venom, he would've done so by now." Fin replied. Weariness tinged her words.

"And what about you?" Emile's voice was softer now, concerned. "Are you recovered enough to travel safely?"

"I'll be fine, Emile. I trust you won't let me slide off the horse if I fall asleep while we ride." She chuckled. There was something in the laugh that gave Alaric strength. She didn't laugh nearly as much as she should, he realized. An idea began to form in his head, pieces of a puzzle falling into place.

"And Alaric? Do you trust him now?"

He heard someone shift. "Yes. I don't know what he remembers, but I saw enough to trust him. Few would do what he did. Even fewer would live through it."

Her words reverberated through his skull, unlocking that which the pain had blocked out. How he'd killed the fighter and ran toward her, intent on getting her to safety like Emile made him swear to do. Seeing the scorpion crawling up the back of the horse. And not caring how many times it jabbed him as he pulled it off and crushed it. The horror on her face as he blacked out. The last thing he saw was her kneeling at his side, the green eyes shifting into gold.

She was Amari.

"Planning on eavesdropping some more, Islander? Or are you ready to admit you're awake?" Emile wasn't quite joking.

Carefully, Alaric sat up. The right arm of his tunic was ripped away at the shoulder, a line of stitches decorated his skin.

"We had Gwen do that. Visual clues of healing are better received by wandering groups over…"

"Over knowing we have an Amari with us? One that's unchained?" Alaric finished Emile's sentence for him.

Fin snorted, "See, Emile? I told you he wasn't stupid."

Emile stared at him, and chose his words carefully. "Now you know. And I know about you, Islander. I don't hire anyone without checking out their background. You need to stay on the move, remain hidden, as much as Fin does. Stay on with us, if you want. We'll protect your secrets as long as you protect her. The minute you betray that, I have no reason not to hand you over to your brother. Or what's left of you."

Alaric nodded, "And what if we mutually decide to part ways?" He knew, the moment he said the words he would never leave Fin's side. But he still had to ask.

Shrugging, Emile responded, "Then we still agree to keep each other's secrets. Fin's lived a life free, Alaric. Much like you have. She's never been anyone's pet, never felt the band of metal enslave her. Make sure it continues, even if our paths move apart, and I promise you'll never have to face your brother unless you choose to."

He looked over at Fin. "Are you agreeable to this?"

She raised her head to meet his gaze. The green coloring was back. "I've trusted Emile for as long as I can remember. He's kept me safe, unchained, this long. If he trusts you, so do I." Turning, her red braid swinging with the movement, Fin started to shove a few things into a pack.

Alaric started to go help her, but a hand on his arm stopped him. Emile smiled, "That's not the way, Islander. She can care for herself in most ways. She's strong, tough. Has needed to be. Don't ever let her think you don't know that." He thrust a chin toward the pallet Alaric had been sleeping on. "Just pack up your bedding and get your gear together. I'll let the others know we're ready to head out."

"Hey, Emile, how long was I out?"

"Three days." Emile disappeared around the open end of the tent.

Alaric blinked, trying to reconnect his thoughts to the lost days. Nothing but pain filled his mind. Shaking his head to clear the thought, he gave up. It wasn't like he could go back and change what happened. Indeed, he probably wouldn't. Three days at the outcropping, though. Emile was right. They had to move onward. Even if they'd kept raiders at bay, there would've been curious travelers.

"Not many, really. One or two, yes. But Gwen would talk to them, get them to move along. No one outside of that first group that gave us any trouble." Fin said.

"Reading my mind?" He joked. And instantly regretted it as her jaw set in a rigid line.

"No, Islander. I don't read minds. I'm not a seer." She didn't even bother to try and hide her irritation.

"Fin, I'm sorry. I didn't mean to imply anything."

She brushed past him, her tightly wrapped bedroll in her arms. "If you don't mean it, don't say it, Islander."

"My name's Alaric." He knotted up the rope, securing his bedding, and rose from the ground.

She was with the pack horse. "Not for a while it's not. Alaric has to disappear for a time. Give your brother time to forget any possible connections between you and Kai. Build up the reputation of an Islander that's good with a bow for now. In a year or so, the connection with your name will be a bowman, not a fugitive."

He nodded. "So, the names you all have. Those are aliases as well?"

She moved back and forth from the tent, bringing out packs and other items and placing them in a pile near the horses. "Bring everything out first, then we load while Trystian and Gwen take down the tent," she instructed.

They worked in silence for a few minutes. Alaric was still curious, but wasn't willing to push the issue. Finally, when everything was out, she began to instruct him on what to bring to her as she loaded up the animal. "Yes and no. Some of us shortened our names out of necessity. Others changed it because we're escaping a life we knew was wrong for us." She strapped a pack into place. "You'll learn what you need to know as we travel, I'm sure. We're all trying to escape something, Islander. In that, the five of us have a common goal."

"More than keeping you free, you mean." He didn't shy away from the statement. Fin's entire speech had been very factual, straightforward. She wasn't one to ignore reality.

She looked over the saddle at him, "Exactly. I don't know all of the stories. Emile does the research, found Gwen and Trystian much as he did you. He makes the decisions. I just follow them. It's easier that way."

He waited until the last item was off the ground, then reached a hand out to touch hers. "If I caused you pain, I apologize. What you did for me...well, I'm grateful."

She slid her hand out from under his and avoided his gaze. "It wasn't bad. It was healing I performed, not harm. My head felt like it was about to split open for a few hours, but no scarring. That only happens when we hurt another."

"Trystian, don't stand under the tent when we're taking it down!" Gwen's exasperated voice called out, jarring Alaric for a moment. He'd forgotten they weren't alone.

No one spoke much while the rest of the camp was torn down. Alaric stayed out of the way, waiting and watching. Everyone knew what to do, trying to help would only result in him getting in the way. So, he kept his eyes open, and dagger out, for more scorpions. They rarely came out during the day, though. But he was wary all the same.

"Islander, what's the chance we meet up with more of the bugs you squashed when we stop tonight?" Trystian called out as the last pole was secured to the pack horse.

Alaric swung up into his saddle. Grasping the reins, he replied, "Slim to none. There's either an oasis or outpost we can stop at each night the rest of the way to the border. We left too late earlier to make it safely or we wouldn't have needed to stop here."

Gwen settled her horse as it pranced, anxious to get moving after the days of inactivity. "What's the situation like at these places?"

Emile answered before Alaric could. "Nothing we haven't encountered before, Gwen. He already told us. Coins in the right hands and no one will know we've passed by."

She snorted, "Not until someone pays more, you mean." She pressed her heels into the animal's flanks and headed toward the road.

Alaric looked toward Emile, who waved him forward. He wanted to talk with Fin more, but it wasn't going to happen as long as she rode with Emile.

Chapter Seven

Dawn broke at some point, but it only changed the shade of grey in the clouds. The rainy season had hit Dunegan's western lands hard. Four months of steady rain, varied only by severity and wind. They'd spent three years in this country, moving every six months or so. Never spending too much time in one village to raise suspicion about Fin. Or any of them for that matter.

Alaric still wasn't thrilled with where Emile wanted them to go next. Lorien. But he hadn't steered them wrong yet. Held up his end of their bargain. It had taken a year to bury the rumor of the lost prince of the Islands. Another for "Islander" to become synonymous with his new name, and skill with a bow. This last year, they'd finally gotten settled in. Trystian had taken up with a young woman in Evenshire, their latest home. Things were encouraging. There were no Amari to be seen. And that meant no slavers waiting to turn Fin into a pet. Or chain Alaric and send him back to face his brother.

Outside of Fin and Emile, no one knew his parentage. He had no clue if Trystian and Gwen knew. If they did, nothing was said. He didn't have the outward signs, did no magic.

Unless you counted his aim. He had grown deadly with his bow, using his marksmanship to both keep them fed and earn their keep as they moved around. The beard was gone, his brown hair longer. Six years on the run now, and his body had changed. He was no longer some soft prince, used to feather beds and savory meals. He was leaner now, more muscle than fat. Wary and suspicious of everyone they met. And, as always, watching out for Fin's safety.

He leaned against the window frame now, alert. Wishing the rain would let up enough they could get back on the road. The others slept on cots behind him. They'd left Evenshire a week ago, after Trystian's lady had begun asking questions. About Fin, Emile. Why he traveled with such companions, took on such danger to protect one person. Emile was fairly certain it was jealousy, but didn't want to wait to have that confirmed. Trystian could've stayed if he wanted to. Instead, he bid his lady good-bye. Told her he'd be back one day, when his task was complete. Alaric knew his companion would keep that vow. He wasn't so certain about the lady.

They got as far as the inn, the last bit of Dunegan hospitality before crossing over to Lorien. The capital was a good month or more west. He prayed Emile would choose to go around the city. Somehow, he doubted it.

"Is it dawn yet?" Fin called out softly from behind him.

Turning, Alaric glanced at her. Her red hair half unbraided, she lay on her cot. Not ready to get up, really, but done sleeping.

"I think so. The clouds are lighter." He kept his voice low so he didn't wake the others.

She threw aside the blanket and sat up, stretching. Her tunic, wrinkled by sleep, hid her slender form. Alaric quickly looked back outside. Thoughts of what might be under that tunic still in his mind.

He heard her moving about, pulling on a pair of trousers. Their life didn't allow for fancy dresses she once told him. It was far more practical to ride in breeches. There was one night, a year ago. A celebration in a town square. She and Gwen had both agreed to dress in borrowed gowns for the event, as they didn't want to anger the man who was letting them stay in the barn and work for a few coins. It was the first time, the only time, he'd seen her dressed up.

The sight of her in the blue dress burned in his mind. A woman's body rested under the corseted top, one that took his breath away.

She leaned against the wall across from him, her fingers deftly undoing the braid. "It's been doing this for days. We're not going to get to Lorien in time if we don't leave soon."

"In time?" he asked. "I didn't know we had a deadline."

Fin shrugged, "It's an anniversary of sorts. Emile and I go back there every ten years. He found me there. I don't know if he's hoping he'll find another to keep free or what, but he's insisted we go back." She finished undoing her hair and shook it loose. "Not that it's a huge thing. This is only the second trip."

"You and Emile have been together since you were three?"

She smiled. "You sound surprised. I think he was about 16 or so. Found me in the sewers. I'd convinced myself that hiding in all the muck would keep me safe."

There was an unspoken rule among the group. No one asked about their lives before they came together. It was as if the past didn't exist before they promised to keep Fin safe. In the quiet of the morning, though, it seemed right.

"Do you remember anything before then? About your parents? Where you lived?"

"No, not really." Her fingers began to braid her hair again. "Vague images of being in a small boat and being very afraid that someone would find me. All my energy went to changing my eyes green for the first few years. Hiding who I am, what I am. So much so that it's instinctive now."

"It's not right, you know. Amari shouldn't have to hide who they are. They should be free like everyone else."

"It's easier for you. I've run into other half Amari. Every one of them had the gold eyes, even if they didn't have the access to magic. You got your father's eyes instead." There was a bitterness to her voice.

"I still feel the same way, Fin. No one should ever be a pet, a slave, to another. The way some force the Amari to use their magic. It's barbaric."

"Like your brother?"

He stared out into the gloomy morning, his jaw clenched. Rumors had reached them over the last few years. Wars fought by Kaerdan and Ajanor, where the Amari dead rivaled the foot soldiers. More and more of the surrounding kingdoms were falling to their forces. And tensions within the alliance grew as well.

Then the news came that Kaerdan's grandfather, the ruler of Lorien, had died after a prolonged illness. His brother now had a major foothold on the mainland that was under his direct control. No more rallying troops under his grandfather's banner. It was his now. And that was a cold reality for Alaric.

"Kaerdan was never one to think of the Amari as anything but a means to an end. For him, that was power." He looked at Fin, "I'm not like him. Even when I didn't know about my real mother. And it's not what he learned from our father."

Her green eyes met his gaze. He still yearned for another glance of the gold. "If Emile ever thought you were, he would've slit your throat while you slept." The steel of her words spoke volumes. Even after these years, the trust wasn't there.

"Don't scare him, Fin." Emile's voice carried from his cot. "He's not stupid. He knows what he signed up for."

A small smile played across Fin's face, the quickest upturn of the lips that Alaric barely caught. Had she been teasing him?

"Emile, there's a shop in town with some archery supplies. I need to restock what I have. What do you think of picking up a bow for Fin?"

She started, interest and fear warring on her face. He turned his head toward the center of the room. "It's a bit too obvious for her to be with us and not have any fighting skills. Anyone would be able to pick her out as the one being protected if we're all combatants and she's not. We get her outfitted with a bow, some flint tipped arrows. I can give her lessons at night during the watch. She may not hit much, but she'll at least look the part."

Emile nodded. "Good idea. I should've thought of that myself." He held up a hand, "Don't argue, Fin. It's decided. The three of us will go right after breakfast. Trystian and Gwen can pack up. Rain or no rain, we head out today."

Alaric watched as Fin eased out of her position on the windowsill. He knew his interest in her was starting to go beyond any sort of promise he made Emile. He wanted to keep her safe now for his own reasons.

Not that she couldn't protect herself. The few times he'd seen her tap into her magic went beyond extraordinary. That he lived through the scorpion's sting still left him in awe. He shuddered to think what Kaerdan would do with her. He'd use her to level entire kingdoms, never caring about the scars or pain it caused her. If his brother ever made a pet of Fin, she'd be dead within a year. Probably less.

And Alaric knew he'd kneel in front of his brother in a heartbeat if it kept her free.

Rising, he casually made his way to his pack. Trystian and Gwen were waking up at Emile's urging. They'd go down as a group, eat. Then he'd lead Emile and Fin the short distance to the shop he'd been told about. He rummaged through his kit, making mental notes about what he needed for himself. Good quality catgut or bowstrings were hard to come by, and expensive, but worth the price. Buy cheap, regret it later when the string breaks when your life depends on it.

"You really think I can shoot a bow?" Fin's voice drifted past his ear.

He turned his head and smiled at her. "Absolutely. It's not that hard. You could even learn how to miss on purpose if you wanted to."

She shrugged, the red hair moving in a way that made him want to reach out and stroke it. "I think I'll be plenty good at missing my target. But you and Emile are right. I need to learn, if for no other reason than to take the attention off of myself." She looked down at her hands. "Any chance I can get some gloves? I've seen the callouses on your hands. They won't happen overnight, and I won't heal myself."

"Why not?" he asked, puzzled. "If I could do what you can, it would make sense to me to do it."

Her mouth turned up slightly, a wistfulness crossing her face. "We can't, Alaric. Amari can do magic, yes. But only to others. Trying to heal myself would be as impossible as it would be for you to shoot yourself in the back. It just can't happen." A small twinkle danced in her green eyes. "And who says you can't do a kind of magic? You may not look like your mother, but your aim is almost inhuman. Surely there's something beyond skill in that."

It was Alaric's turn to shrug. "Who can say, really? Even if there's a bit more to it than skill, I don't have any of your disadvantages. I can kill without scars."

"You aren't doing the killing. The arrow is. There's a difference." Her tone echoed a despair he couldn't really fathom.

"Fin, you don't have to answer this. But...have you?"

"Have I ever killed someone? No. Not yet. I've come close, but Emile stepped in first. But I do have scars. Some hurt more than others when I got them."

He knew better than to pursue the topic. A sadness radiated from her now, making his heart ache. The last thing he wanted was to hurt her.

The rest of the morning passed in silence. Everyone knew what had to be done before starting to travel again, and each had their own duties. Right after breakfast, Emile nodded to Fin and him and the three headed to the archery place. Trystian and Gwen would either meet them outside, or back here if the pack horse was still being loaded.

The wooden overhang gave them the chance to shake some rain off their cloaks before entering the shop. A steady stream of pale smoke rose from the brick chimney, giving Alaric notice that the shop would be warm. A good sign for a bowmaker. Constant damp and cool while shaping the wood would warp it past use.

A small bell rang out as Emile opened the door. A fireplace took up most of one wall, heating the shop effectively. A tall man, blue eyes peering out from beneath shaggy grey eyebrows, watched them enter. Emile leaned against the doorway. Alaric knew the man well enough to see the stance wasn't nearly as relaxed as he looked.

"My friend here," he placed a hand on Fin's shoulder, "wants to take up the bow."

The shop owner looked her up and down. "Don't know that I'd start you off with a longbow like your friend, miss. Recommend something a bit shorter. Get used to the flow of the weapon before you move into something with more punch."

He moved around the workbench, waving a hand over toward a small assortment of bows leaning against the far wall. The artisan didn't ask questions, simply began to show her various things. In less than an hour, they were back out into the rain. Alaric had the supplies he needed. And Fin was ready to learn what a bow could do.

Trystian and Gwen sat on their horses, waiting. "Get everything?" Trystian asked.

Emile nodded as he mounted his horse. "And Alaric didn't even spend all my gold." Reaching down, he lifted Fin up into the saddle in front of him. "Rain or no rain, we head to Lorien. I've got an appointment to keep."

Alaric touched his heels to his horse's flanks, urging it to follow his companions.

Chapter Eight

The capital looked different than he remembered it. The white stone no longer reflected the afternoon sun. Instead, it was a dull grey, lifeless, and bare of the green vegetation that'd been there six years earlier. Soot from forges blanketed the streets. Kaerdan's war machine was in full swing.

Emile stopped. "Things have changed." His words conveyed the same concern Alaric had. He whispered something in Fin's ear, and she slowly eased out of her customary spot in front of him. "Alaric, Fin's going to ride in with you. If anyone asks, she's your betrothed and her horse went lame."

Nodding, he reached down to help Fin up into his saddle. She settled in against him, making his heart race. "Can I ask why?"

Emile turned back to him, "I'm too old to be marrying her. Trystian wears the token of another. At her age now, she needs to be protected in that way. Your brother's let his army take over the city. If she's not attached, they'd consider her fair bait." He paused. "You've got a nephew, Alaric. That's why we're in town. To pay homage to the newborn prince." Sarcasm dripped from his voice. "Let me do the talking. We go directly to a place I know that's safe. Only then do we do anything else." He smiled grimly. "I wouldn't go bragging about the relationship if I were you, though."

Emile's warning brought Alaric back to his senses, and the feel of Fin's body next to his became less of a distraction. "Don't worry, Emile. I'll be avoiding the spotlight."

Following the older man, the group made their way toward the city gates. Alaric didn't even try to hear the exchange between the guards. He felt Fin's body tense up as their gaze passed over to her. Thinking swiftly, he placed a quick kiss on the top of her head while meeting their gaze. Satisfied, the guard made notes on a piece of paper while Emile handed the other one some coins. Once the transaction was complete, the guards waved them onward and moved to the next in the line.

Emile led them through the crowded streets. Litter and mud cluttered the drainage lines, causing an overflow into the streets. The paved stones no longer cleaned by anything but the rain. The houses and shops were in varying stages of decay, as well. This didn't surprise Alaric much. Kaerdan never cared much for how those in the village around their father's castle lived back on the island. He thought Erien would've done more, though. She'd been so caring, so conscientious, back in Antioch. Though there was a good chance that marriage to Kaerdan had changed her. He shoved the thought from his head. That his friend would change her nature that drastically scared him.

By the time Emile stopped them in front of an inn whose owner took pride in its' appearance, Alaric shuddered. He knew things couldn't be good for Erien, and his brother wouldn't see the suffering. But that they allowed the populace of their capital slide into the despair and misery he'd seen shook his very soul.

The inside showed some changes even Alaric didn't expect. The common room was divided by a heavy tapestry, with a large man stationed at the end. "Ladies must go to the right," he intoned as he gestured. "This is a proper establishment. The house ladies will attend to them while you check in this way." His right arm pointed to Alaric's left.

Emile bowed slightly. "We mean no disrespect, good sir, to either the owner or his family. However, I would prefer my daughter and her companion remain with us. This gentleman," he put a hand on Alaric's shoulder, "is her betrothed. I can assure you that nothing improper would occur should we have adjoining rooms."

The large man shook his head. "If they were husband and wife, it would not matter. We follow the rules set down by the new Queen, ones that have consequences if not obeyed."

Gwen put her arms around Fin's slender shoulders. "I will watch over her, Master Amain." She used a name Emile had in the past. One of his many aliases. "Do not fear for her safety." Without another word, the two women disappeared between the hanging swaths of dark silk.

Alaric watched them depart, then looked at Emile for a clue of what to do next. The other man's face seemed relaxed and unconcerned, but his jaw was tight. A brief nod passed between them before heading through the other entrance.

The dark wood tables and chairs gleamed in the warm firelight in the room. Few patrons sat at the tables or bar that dominated the other side of the room. An older man stopped wiping at the counter. "Master Amain! My friend! It has been too long!" His greeting to Emile seemed genuine, not forced, as he moved around the bar.

"Grendal! Too long, you're right." He embraced the other man.

Laughing, the men broke apart. "What of your daughter, Sera? She is well, I hope?"

"Indeed. She is next door," he gestured to the heavy tapestry splitting the room in half. "But I don't understand. It was never an issue before for us to have adjoining rooms."

"It's the queen, Amain. She and the king—" Grendal spat on the ground, "—they do not get along well. She has enacted certain laws so that women are protected from the likes of his soldiers. If an establishment follows the laws voluntarily, any kingsman who disrupts the women's quarters is dealt with swiftly and severely. But have no fear. I will put you in a room where you can still communicate with her." He clasped Emile's shoulder. "Now, who are your friends?"

Emile smiled, "Tyrone and Alaric. One's good at keeping us safe as we travel, the other is Sera's betrothed. I'll let you figure out which is which." He laughed.

"Welcome, friends. If you travel with Master Amain, you are safe here. Come. Your journey, no doubt, has been a long one. I'm sure you wish for a good rest, better food, and perhaps clean clothes." He grabbed at a set of keys hanging on the wall. "Namine runs the women's side for me. I'm certain Sera and her companion are being well taken care of already. I will take you up to your room and you will be able to know for yourself."

They followed Grendal up the staircase, the older man far more spry than Alaric expected. He stopped before a room at the end of the hall. "This room was set up for instances like yours, Amain. I'm sure you'll feel all is well soon." He handed a key to Emile. "I'll have someone bring up meals in about an hour." The man brushed past Alaric as he headed back down the stairs.

Alaric caught a look on Trystian's face, and looked back at Emile. He moved a single finger to his lips, signaling for silence. Alaric eased a dagger out of the sheath at the small of his back as Trystian moved toward the door. He didn't know what was on the other side, but Emile's cautious stance made him more than wary. But he knew the man wasn't buying Grendal's reasons.

He watched, his thumb nervously caressing the hilt of his dagger, as Emile waited for Trystian to take up position in front of the door. The older man grasped the doorknob firmly. When Trystian nodded his readiness, Emile twisted the handle and threw the door open in a fluid motion. Alaric followed Trystian as he charged into the room.

"The theatrics weren't necessary, Alaric. I've known you were coming for a week or more now." A female voice called out from a ring of chairs in front of a fireplace.

He stopped. Gwen and Fin sat facing him, their faces a mask. He didn't need the other woman to turn around. He'd recognized Erien's voice the moment she spoke.

Emile broke the silence. "Hello, Your Majesty. To what do we owe this honor?"

She rose, as graceful as Alaric remembered. His heart sank when he saw the bitterness on her face. The softness replaced with a stony coldness. She'd changed. Or Kaerdan had changed her.

"You can drop the pretense, Emile. I know who you all are. What you are." She didn't even try to disguise the threat. "We can make this easy, or hard. I only need to have a word or three with Kai." Alaric started at her use of his old name. "Alone. Once that discussion is complete, I'll go the way I came in. None need know I was here. Or you were, for that matter."

"And if we don't agree?" Emile had moved closer toward Fin. Alaric knew he'd try to grab her and run. And that Gwen and Trystian would provide cover for their escape.

"It's fine. I agree." Alaric spoke. He locked his gaze with Emile's. "I'm willing to talk. And listen. Provided I have your guarantee my companions will not be harmed or detained in any way while we do."

A tired smile crossed Erien's face. "But of course. You have my word as Queen."

Emile and Fin looked at each other, then the older man nodded once. "I take it the door over there leads to the women's half of the room?" Alaric watched as Gwen led

Fin toward the door. Trystian followed. Emile gave him one last look before he departed and closed the door behind him. Alaric knew he'd be listening in as best he could.

He turned back towards Erien. "What do you—" his question was interrupted as she flew into his arms, kissing him.

For a brief moment, he enjoyed the feel of her lips on his. Her body clung to him. It wasn't right, though. And he knew it. No matter how many times he'd longed for her to come to him when they lived in Antioch, this wasn't right. He broke free of the kiss, only to have her bury her head in his chest, arms locked tight around his waist.

"I've missed you so much," she whispered. "Every night, I go to sleep wishing I could turn back time and run off like you suggested. Honor be damned, I should've listened to you."

"But you didn't, Erien. Is this why you wanted to see me?"

She pulled away slightly, but did not fully let go of him. Raising her head, her eyes locked with his. "I can't leave him. I know that. But give me one night, Kai. One that I can take with me every time your brother comes to my chamber drunk. A memory I can treasure. Then you and your friends can take your pet and go." Her hand began to pull at his shirt.

Disgusted, he pushed her hand away and grabbed at her wrists. "My name's not Kai. It's Alaric. And Fin is no one's pet." His voice echoed harshly in his own ears.

Confusion ruled Erien's face for a moment. Then, her eyes widened in shock. "You love her."

Alaric let go of her wrists and walked around a chair. Leaning on the back, he exhaled slowly. "It's complicated, Erien."

She laughed, but there wasn't any mirth in it. "You love her, and she doesn't love you. Or you can't gather the courage up to tell her." She sneered at him, "Kaerdan's terrified of you, and you're letting some Amari witch control you. All you would need to do is raise your hand and the entire kingdom could be yours. He's a bully. The people know it. And they're tired of his brutality." She crossed the room toward him. "I'd be yours, as well. Challenge him to a duel and you win me. You win a kingdom. I'd even let you keep that one as a pet if you must. But don't think for a moment you can turn your back on me and walk away, Kai. You're destined for so much more than some mercenary with a bow."

"I swore an oath, Erien. To keep her safe and out of chains. I'm not going to turn my back on that for any reason." His fingers grasped the chair firmly. "Kai's dead. He and I were on the same boat, yes. But he died. I saw him be buried at sea. Kaerdan has no fear that his half Amari brother is going to show up to challenge his rule." Inhaling deeply, he weighed his next words carefully, knowing they would be the most painful for her to hear. "I'm not sleeping with you, Erien. I'd rather find myself in chains kneeling before your husband than give up Fin."

Shock played across her face, followed by grief. He'd once thought he loved her, yes. A few years ago, he would've jumped at what she offered. But that was then. He'd changed too much.

She was right about something, though. He loved Fin. The idea of betraying her, even if she never looked at him that way, chilled his very soul. Any hope of a relationship with her rested on her choices, her terms. He wasn't about to jeopardize his chances with Fin. She had a very good memory.

Erien's face became a stone mask, unreadable and unyielding. "I give you two days, Alaric." Her voice, defeated, was barely above a whisper. "Conclude your business and quickly. I won't stop him from finding you or your friends."

Without another word, she turned and slid aside a panel of the wall. A man stood there, gold eyes reflecting the torch he carried. "Take me back to the palace," she said.

The Amari stepped aside to allow her to pass, then closed the door behind her. Alaric turned the chair around in one swift motion, falling into it without a thought. His heart raced. Did he just condemn them all to being hunted?

He heard the others come back into the room, but continued to stare into the fire. He wasn't sure if he was numb or overwhelmed knowing that Erien's life was beyond any horror he might have imagined. Kaerdan sober was bad enough. Drunk would've been even uglier.

"We have two days. I say we leave in one." Emile's voice pierced the fog in his head. "Fin and I will do what we must tonight. We leave again at first light."

At some point, Gwen handed him a plate with food on it. "Eat," she commanded. "Emile's going to move us fast for a few days. He'll want to get us out of Lorien lands sooner rather than later."

"Shouldn't worry yourself too much about your lady friend, Alaric," Trystian's voice stayed low. "She's a survivor. If she couldn't handle her life, she would've been dead by now." Alaric heard the scrape of a whetstone across the large man's blade. "You did good, turning her down. She'd have sunk her claws in deep and had you leading a rebellion if you'd slept with her."

"What is so important that Emile and Fin had to come back here?" Alaric asked, not really expecting an answer.

"Twenty years ago, he found Fin. In a sewer here in Lorien. She was really young, maybe five years old, and thought she could hide. Barely knew how to keep her eyes hidden. Before he took her out, he left a message down there. Promising to come back with her every ten years. So her family would know when they could find her again, or any other unchained Amari knew when help would be there."

Alaric switched his chair around, facing Trystian. The other man sat calmly on a sofa, sharpening his blade with even strokes.

"Have her parents ever come? Or another Amari?"

Trystian shrugged, "No. I hadn't been with them long when we came back the first time. Fin was still fairly young then. Hadn't learned to guard her emotions like she can now. Tore her up to leave without anyone. Not even a sigil left behind saying her parents had even gone down there."

"She changed not long after that," Gwen spoke up. "Stopped hoping, began to see us as her family. If anyone was there tonight, I think she'd be cautious before accepting their word as truth. We've had too many close calls. She's seen how easily other Amari fall prey to slavers who pretend to be something they're not."

The sound of the secret door opening up alerted them all. Trystian and Gwen took up a ready stance while Alaric grabbed at his bow. If he could string it fast enough, he might get a shot in.

A woman stepped into the room, her head lowered. Short brown hair and a slight frame. A thin band of metal encircled her wrist.

"Holly?" Alaric said, stunned.

She raised his head. "My mistress sends word. She has been summoned by His Majesty, to answer for her whereabouts earlier today. She regrets to inform you she may not be able to give you the full time promised." Silently, Holly retreated back through the hidden passage.

Alaric looked at Trystian and Gwen. "Gwen, grab their packs. We'll meet them at the exit," Trystian's beard shook as he spoke. "Alaric, keep that bow strung. We may need it yet."

Within minutes, the trio had everything in hand. "There's a back staircase. Emile used it to go out with Fin." Gwen motioned to them from the connecting door. "We should be fine using it. He wouldn't have taken her that way if it wasn't safe."

Alaric shrugged, adjusting his pack on his shoulders. "Go. I'll take up the rear." With Gwen leading the way, the three of them made their way down the staircase quickly.

Trystian moved to the front, easing the door to the alleyway open. Peering outside, he motioned for them to follow. Alaric glanced behind once, making sure no one followed them.

The passage was narrow and dark. Rats chittered amongst the trash as they passed through. "Gwen," Trystian whispered, "we don't have time to get the horses. Leave them. Head to the stables, grab the larger packs with the tents. Meet us at the exit."

Gwen nodded once, then disappeared down a small passage. A sliver of a moon gave a little light as Alaric followed Trystian through a maze of back streets. He knew they were being hunted.

As they turned a corner, the castle on top of the city came into view. Alaric paused, his feet moving almost involuntarily toward the bright light burning from a single window of the complex. Erien was up there, with Kaerdan. And his brother most likely wasn't being kind.

"Your friend's either talking by now, or in a world of pain. She gave us the chance to escape. Honor her sacrifice by taking it." Trystian's gruff voice echoed in his ear.

Shaking off the feeling, Alaric turned his back on the path leading to the keep. In his heart, he closed the door that led to Erien at the same time.

Soldiers were beginning to search for them now. They kept to shadows and back alleys, moving in bursts of speed. Alaric's mind filled with thoughts of Fin. He and Trystian had to get there unseen. If they didn't, if they were followed…

"Keep your mind on the task at hand, Islander." Trystian growled at him as his large arm flattened Alaric against a wall. "If it's a choice between you and Fin, you know who I'll save."

A small patrol, maybe four or five troops, jogged past the alley where they hid. Alaric had almost stepped in front of them. Trystian was right. He shook his head, clearing away the worry and concern. Fin's safety was what mattered, not what might happen to him. "Sorry," he muttered.

After several blocks, they came to a dark courtyard. The paving stones beneath his feet became slick with muck. Three exposed pipes jutted out of walls, sewage and waste overtaking the bottom quarter of each tube. Trystian leaned against one wall and motioned Alaric to take up a position on the opposite side of the courtyard. Anyone coming out of those pipes would now either meet Trystian's sword or Alaric's bow.

He kept an eye on the alley they'd come down. It bent between the street and their location, so he didn't have a clear light of sight. Instead, he willed his heart to slow down and listened for any sound beyond the rats running about.

A whistled note pierced the quiet. Trystian answered in kind. Alaric lowered his bow as Gwen emerged from the dark.

"Not out yet?" she whispered.

Trystian shook his head, then jutted his chin to the point on the wall he wanted her to take up. "It's early yet. They don't know what's going on. We wait."

For the next hour, they stood. Not speaking. Listening and waiting. Alaric's legs didn't bother him. Not yet. But he knew the muscles in his back weren't going to be happy when they finally stopped running.

His body was still, but his mind raced. He knew he'd not hesitate to surrender himself if that's what it took to get Fin out safely. Then again, he couldn't trust any promise Kaerdan might make. The minute his brother knew about Fin, she would become a weapon to be used against Alaric. He'd need to make sure she got out of town first. If he was lucky, he'd be able to go with her.

"Stop that thought, Alaric." Gwen's voice drifted to him. "Only way we get out of here is if we all do."

A rustling came from one of the pipes. Alaric's hand flew to his quiver, drawing out an arrow. It was notched and ready to fly before Emile emerged.

"She's right, Alaric. If we have to go, we all go," the older man commented as he climbed free of the pipe. Gwen knelt down and reached her arm in, helping pull Fin free of the small space. "If you three are here, it means we leave tonight." Emile didn't even wait for an explanation. He went over to the pile of packs Gwen had deposited on the ground. Rummaging through the stack, he tossed one over to Fin. "We head north. Caerlynn's got a new ruler. Rumor has it he's allowing the Amari to live normal lives."

"Met someone this time?" Trystian kept his voice low.

"No, but someone had left word." Emile shouldered his pack and one of the tents. "There's a way out of the city, but it'll be tricky. Stay close." He slid down the other alleyway, not looking back.

Alaric waited for the others to follow and took up the rear. Fin and Emile both were covered in sludge from the sewer, but moved quickly.

Emile led them through a few more side streets, deftly avoiding patrols and drunks. Finally, he stopped them at the back door of a house. Laughter, punctuated by screaming, poured from the open windows. His mind rebelled against what was probably going on inside.

"Gwen, Fin, keep your heads down. If anyone asks, you belong to us. Don't speak, just point to one of us. Women aren't expected to speak in this house unless given permission by whoever paid for them that night." Emile looked at Alaric. "You'll need to act like you own one of them. Don't let what you'll see get under your skin. If they even suspect you're half Amari, they'll put you under the same rules they would Fin or Gwen. We won't be in here long. I hope." He turned and knocked once.

The door opened. Bright candlelight made the person in the doorway barely recognizable. His bulk, however, wasn't as easy to hide. "Full up tonight if you're buying. Or are you selling?"

"Neither. I need to see Paul." Emile spoke.

The doorman squinted, trying to make them out. "No one sees Paul unless he knows they're coming. And he didn't tell me you were expected."

Emile rummaged about in his tunic, pulling a small item out of a hidden pocket. Alaric couldn't tell what it was. "Give him this," he put it in the bouncer's hand. "If he still won't see us, I'll be surprised."

The large man stared at the item in his hand. "I know what it is. He'll want to see you." He pointed at Gwen and Fin. "Keep the wenches under control. If they're mistaken for workers, we aren't held responsible for damages." He turned around and gestured at them to follow him.

The main room was filled with men and a few women. Most of the women wore little except for the metal band around their necks. A few of the men were in the same condition. For a pleasure house, it was relatively clean. From the screams coming from above them, that's where most of the business was conducted.

Their guide stopped on the other side of the room before an iron bound door. "Wait here," he intoned, then lifted the bar and went inside.

"How come they're hiding the red-haired one?" A drunk voice bellowed from across the room.

Alaric moved between the man staggering toward Fin. "Because she's already paid for."

The man swayed on his feet, inches away from Alaric's face. Sweat poured down his ruddy cheeks, the odor combining with the ale to make him truly reek. "Ain't no Amari whore that can't be paid for more than once. What's your price?"

Without thinking, Alaric drew his dagger and put it under the drunk's chin. "She's no Amari, you fool. No chain on her, no gold eyes. And I paid dearly for first rights. You won't see enough coin in your entire life to come close to having enough." He shoved the drunk away from them.

He lost his footing, falling flat on the floor. The man's eyes narrowed, "Watch what you do, boy. I ain't afraid of you. If I want something, I get it. You can get some coin out of it, or not."

Another man stepped in front of Alaric, a quarterstaff at the ready. "Not in my house, Damien. This man's paid for her, she's his. Get your drunk ass out of here. And take your crew with you. Not taking your money tonight."

The other man rose, shooting a hate-filled glance at Alaric. He pulled two other men away from the women they were fondling and headed to the exit.

"Sorry, Emile. Sometimes Damien forgets his manners around here." He pointed his staff towards the open door. "This way. Let's get you on the road before anyone else gets stupid."

Alaric followed down a passageway. The bouncer nodded once when he passed through the open door, then closed it behind him. He heard the heavy bar being placed back over the door.

"I don't like coming here, Paul. But the need was urgent tonight."

"I understand, my friend. Rumor runs rampant. Half my clientele for the night went in search of your archer friend there. And the unchained Amari." The man with the quarterstaff responded. "I owe you quite a bit. I daresay we might be even after tonight."

Emile chuckled, "Oh, probably. That drunk's not going to cause you problems later on, is he?"

"Damien? Nah. He and his crew like to pretend they can spot an Amari by sight. They're wrong more than they're right. Militia knows that. Even if he went to them right now and said he knew where your group was at, they wouldn't believe him." Paul stopped under a torch, giving Alaric his first real look at the man.

Slightly built and closely cropped blonde hair, he was fairly unremarkable. But his hands grasped the weapon in such a way that Alaric knew he'd be dangerous in a fight.

"You know the way from here, right?" Paul asked Emile. "I need to get back. Need to keep things moving smoothly."

Emile nodded. "Thanks, my friend. I won't be back this way again."

Paul brushed past the group and headed back toward the common area.

Emile worked aside one brick in the wall, revealing a small opening. He reached inside. The wall in front of them began to move, a small shower of dirt falling as it shifted.

"We go out this way," Emile stated as he lifted the torch out of the ring on the wall. "Keep close. The ground's uneven. When we get the door closed, we'll find another torch to give us a little more light."

"How far is it?" Fin asked.

"Far enough that we'll spend at least one night in here. And be at the edge of Kaerdan's reach when we come out." The man waved them on to pass through the portal.

Alaric ducked through the opening, not wanting to go far into the enveloping dark. The musty aroma of earth surrounded him.

Emile pushed down on a lever sticking out of the stone near the door, and it slid back into place.

"Now what, Emile?" Fin spoke from near Alaric. The darkness was so deep he'd not realized how close she was.

"We get another torch lit, and walk. There's a pool of fresh water up ahead. We can camp there for tonight. Rest. Get cleaned up. No one's going to bother us in here."

Gwen's face brightened as the torch in her hand caught some of the flame from Emile's. She passed it on to Alaric. "One in the front, one in the back. Let's move."

Slowly, they made their way through the darkness. He didn't know how long they'd be in the dark, but swore he'd get Fin practicing with her bow once they were above ground again.

He lost track of time. The only thing keeping him from going mad was the flickering torch he held, matched by the one Emile held up ahead of him. The meager light kept whatever might be hiding in the dark at bay.

Alaric never had issues with the dark before the scorpion sting. Since then, though, things had changed slightly. His encounter with the total blackness of death changed him. He knew what was out there, waiting for him. He'd escaped death once, thanks to Fin. And now it waited for the chance to strike again.

Emile stopped, his torch no longer moving as he did. As Alaric approached, the walls opened up around him. The cavern's walls, decorated with veins of quartz, reflected the torchlight. A small river flowed through one side. Clear water collected in a small pool in the center before disappearing through another opening. "We stop here for the night," Emile stated. "We can fill up our water skins, clean up in the pool. Get some sleep."

No one needed to be told anything else. The routine of setting up camp began. Bedrolls came out, but not the tents. Trystian got a fire started and rummaged about for ingredients for that night's dinner. Gwen and Fin went to the far side of the pond to fill up water stores and bathe. Alaric resisted the urge to watch. The light wasn't enough where he'd see anything, but felt they should still have some privacy. The splash, followed immediately by a shocked squeal, made him turn his head though.

Fin was standing waist deep in the water. Her hands pushed water from her hair, giving him a tantalizing view of her naked profile. The shadows kept details hidden, but not enough to keep his loins from tightening at the sight. "No peeking, Islander," Trystian whispered from the fire. "Best not let either of them know you saw anything. They're strong women. Stronger than most. And Fin's just as likely to castrate you as anything. They make the choices, not us."

Alaric turned away and moved closer to the fire. Trystian was right. Any relationship he might have with Fin would be because she chose it.

Chapter Nine

The light ahead grew larger as they approached. But also fainter. Emile had warned them they'd reach the end of the tunnel today, but wouldn't be able to leave it. That would wait for dawn. When they could emerge without giving away the location and still have a full day to travel.

"We keep watch tonight, no fires." Emile extinguished his torch and motioned at Alaric to do the same. "Few know of this route, and it must be kept that way."

Alaric took a wistful look at the rapidly fading light. The smell of fresh air teased his nose. That was something, at least. One more night and he'd be out under the open sky again.

They moved quickly, before it became too dark to see. No sense to do much beyond pass around some bread or dried beef. Alaric found a section of the wall that wasn't too rocky and settled in to sleep.

Someone or something nudged his foot, rousing him. Emile stood over him. "Your turn," he whispered. Alaric rose, taking in what little he could see. The moon was full, giving them a faint light. Trystian slept, his sword in his hand. Gwen and Emile both grabbed at blankets, ready to rest. Fin silently folded hers before tying it to her pack.

Alaric walked toward her, avoiding both his sleeping companions and their gear. "I don't think we'll be shooting tonight," he said, keeping his voice light.

Fin snorted, "You think?" she replied sarcastically. "Trying to be funny, Islander?"

Her tone stung. "Not really, Fin. Just making conversation."

She scrambled up on a rock close enough to the exit to observe, but not be seen. "It's not you, Alaric. It's this tunnel. The darkness. I hate it."

He took up a position opposite of her. "I understand that. It's oppressive in a lot of ways. I've felt like death was waiting for me since we first came in here. But I've had issues with darkness ever since that damn scorpion bit me."

"That's natural, I suppose. At least you know where your fear comes from. That's half way to conquering it. I don't know." She plucked a small patch of moss off of the wall next to her, picking it to pieces as she spoke. "I've been in this tunnel before. The sewers where Emile found me were dark, but I was more afraid then of the light. Because that meant someone was coming to chain me, make me their pet. The dark was a good thing."

"So, what's changed?"

Fin threw the remains of the moss towards the sheltered opening. It bounced against the bushes blocking the way out, finally coming to rest on a rather nasty looking thorn. "Maybe it's me that's changed. Maybe I'm tired of hiding, being on alert all the time. Never able to relax." She let out a heavy sigh. "I've been hiding for over twenty years, Alaric. No one should have to do that just to stay free."

A single tear wove a path down her face, catching the moonlight. Alaric rose, crossing the small space to be closer to her. "So, stop hiding. When it's just the five of us. You can relax. We won't treat you any differently, won't put a leash on you," he whispered. His heart broke to hear her vocalize her pain. Even though he was living a life hidden himself, it wasn't to her extent. He didn't have to hide his eyes just to stay alive.

She didn't reply, and wouldn't look at him. Her head turned toward the brambles. Alaric moved back to his spot on the opposite side. And kept the watch in silence.

Three hours later, when the light began to shift, Fin spoke again. "It's time. Let's wake the others and get moving."

Alaric nodded, easing his way off the small ledge he'd perched on. While Fin got the rest up, he shouldered his pack and adjusted the quiver on his hip. He preferred to keep the bow unstrung, but decided to have it ready just in case. There was no way of knowing what they'd encounter when they left.

He did a quick survey of the area once Emile moved toward the exit, making sure nothing was left behind. As he turned back around, Fin was there. Her green eyes gold for the first time in weeks. She stretched up, planting a gentle kiss on his cheek. "Thank you," she whispered.

He smiled, resisting the urge to pull her into him. "What did I do right?"

"You listened." With those words, her eyes reverted back to the green she let the world see. The mask back in place, she followed the others out of the cave.

Still smiling, Alaric followed. Tonight, he'd have to find the carcass of an animal if he could. Teach her the difference between hitting trees and flesh with her arrows. And maybe she'd allow him into her world a little bit more.

Chapter Ten

"Pretty sure you know what happened after that," he added.

The sun had set over an hour ago, leaving the two of them in shadows on the porch. The old woman had left, but something told Alaric that he shouldn't go back inside. Not yet.

Christoph whistled, "Well, then. I can see why you hid out under another name. If Kaerdan ever knew I was harboring his brother…"

"He won't, though. If he put it together, even after torturing his own wife, he'd have crossed your border and put this place to the torch by now."

"Think he's waiting for something?"

Alaric shrugged, "He's always been an opportunist. You're smart to keep an eye on him. Lorien and Antioch are not getting along well currently. He's more concerned with that squabble. No offense, Christoph, but your kingdom's small. Not a lot of land. And he's probably scared to death that you've got unchained Amari that will fight willingly. They're not simply doing it because they have to. They'd tear apart any army he brought here because they're defending their homes. They didn't get to do that in the caves, but they will this time."

A scream pierced the night, coming from inside the house. Alaric jumped up, "Fin!" he called as he ran into their home.

She knelt on the floor, her red hair concealing her face. Lyssa knelt next to her. A puddle of water spread out underneath her. The leather journal the old woman had given her was clasped tightly in one of Fin's hands. The other rested on her distended belly.

Rushing over to her, he fell to his knees. "What's wrong?" he demanded as he moved her hair away from her face.

"Nothing, Alaric." Lyssa's voice was calm, almost amused. "Help me get her up and to your bed. Then, have Christoph summon the midwife."

He stared at her, uncomprehending.

"Alaric, I'm in labor," Fin panted out. "Do what she tells you. Now is not a time to argue with a woman."

Reaching down, he put one arm underneath hers and eased her up off the floor. With Lyssa's help, he guided Fin into the other room and onto the bed. As she sank onto the mattress, he took the book she clutched out of her hand. "I'll go tell Christoph to find the midwife," he said, placing the journal onto a small side table. "I'll be right back."

Dashing out of the room, he almost collided with his friend in the doorway. "She's in labor. Lyssa said—"

"I know. I heard." Christoph replied, interrupting him. "Go back in there and be with Fin. Do whatever she needs you to do. I'll keep the curious at bay."

"Curious?" Alaric asked, puzzled.

Christoph smiled. "Your child is the first Amari in some time to be born to parents that have never known slavery. At least, the first we know of. They've been respectful of you both, but your child gives many here hope for their own future. To them, he or she is a gift." Fin let out another scream. "Go. Be with your wife. That's where you're needed now."

Alaric nodded, and clasped the King's hand in friendship briefly before heading back into the bedroom.

"The midwife's on her way," he said. Fin lay back, her face pained. "What can I do?"

Lyssa lifted a cloth out of a bowl of water. Wringing out the excess, she folded it neatly and placed it across Fin's forehead. "Fin, where do you want Alaric to be?"

She pointed to a chair near the bed. "Bring that closer. And grab the book." Her breathing began to return to normal.

Alaric grasped the chair in one hand and pulled it closer to the side of the bed. With his free hand, he took the book off the table. "What do you want me to do with this?" he asked, waving the book slightly as he sat in the chair.

"Read it to me."

Opening the small drawer in the table next to the bed, he brought out a couple more candles. One by one, he lit them and placed them on the plate next to the others. "Gotta make sure I can see," he told her.

Leaning back, he opened the book and began to read aloud.

Serafina,

Today, our lives changed. Today, your mother died to save you. And so will I, in the years ahead, in order to keep you safe.

Today, the humans brought war to Uamh nan Amari, our home. And I started the charade that will be the only way I can keep you in my life. Know you, raise you.

When I left the caves in search of you, I was Grear. Cousin to Artemis, King. And your father.

When I find you, I will be Emile. And will hide that I am your father from you. I will lie to you, steal for you, protect you with every breath I take.

If you're reading this journal, then those lies have caught up with me. I can only hope you're safe now. I will never know. Nor will your mother.

In the years to come, I'll write in this journal. Things I wanted to say as your father and couldn't. Of our adventures, both good and bad. Maybe one day you'll forgive me for the deception.

G.

Book Three:

Emile's Blade

For my Dad.
Who taught me love, respect, ethics, and sacrifice.
I miss you.

Chapter One

Grear darted past the streams of people fleeing the caves. The amassed forces of five separate kingdoms bore down on their home, intent on rounding up the last free home the Amari had.

"Grear! To me!" A voice screamed at him over the crowd. Looking toward the sound, he saw an arm beckoning him. As quickly as he could, he wove through the throng and found the uniformed man who called to him.

"What is it?" he asked, his breath coming in gasps. "My family…are they alright?"

The blonde man nodded his head, the gold eyes darting past Grear's head to survey the crowd. "I'm sure they're fine. Artemis needs you."

He shook his head emphatically. "No. I have to get to Bella and Serafina. Tell him he can find me at the rendezvous spot and impart his kingly wisdom there!"

A hand reached out, grabbing his arm. "Grear, it's set in motion. Bella took her to the river already."

The blood rushed out of his face as fear settled on his heart. "Lead the way," he said, his voice wooden and heavy.

The other man wove a path through a series of caverns and tunnels, avoiding as many people as possible. "The raid started earlier than we thought it would," he spoke over his shoulder. "Artemis got Lyssa into hiding, and summoned Bella as soon as he ordered us to evacuate."

Grear didn't answer. It was too late for talk, too late to say goodbyes.

They stopped in front of a plain looking set of double doors. "He's in there. Refuses to leave. Says it's not part of the plan." He reached out his hand to Grear. "Take care of yourself. Stay free. Or try to."

Grear took it in the friendship it was offered. "You as well, Titus."

As Titus disappeared down the corridor, he pushed open the doors in front of him.

Artemis stood at the far end, his back to Grear. The sheer curtains that kept the sitting room separate from the balcony had been pushed aside. Ignoring the shelves of books, he strode past the leather chairs and finely carved tables.

"Might as well grab yourself a drink, Grear," Artemis' deep voice called out. "You'll need one soon enough."

He hesitated, the amber liquid in the crystal decanter tempting. "No, Artemis. I don't need a drink. I need to know why you gave the order before I could say goodbye to them." He walked out to the balcony and leaned against the rail. And waited for an answer.

Artemis stepped back from the edge, his hands resting on the barrier. He kept his focus on the people below fleeing Uamh nan Amari. "It was time. If we waited for you, we would've lost the opportunity. The humans will be on us soon. Most of our people will be rounded up as they leave the caves. If the ruse is to work, it had to happen when it did." He turned, "I'm sorry, cousin. I really am. I know this will be hard on you. Raising her without any knowledge of who she is, what she is, who you are. And now she'll think her father is dead."

"What about Bella?" he whispered.

"She'll remain at the river, as planned. When they find her, she'll give them the story of how the last royal for my household is far from their grasp. Everyone will think it's my own daughter." He took a deep breath. "Given the magic she's going to harness to send Fin downriver safely, she won't live long enough to be chained. You'll never encounter her as someone's pet. Fin won't have to see it, either."

Grear's heart constricted. His wife had agreed to this. He did, as well. It was the only way to ensure both Fin's safety and the continuation of the royal line. But, now that the events were in motion, it cut deeper than any wound he'd ever gotten.

Artemis placed a hand on his shoulder. "They're going to take me, Grear. They'll make me tell them everything. I can only say I saw your wife leave with your daughter and you went after them. Make me believe, now, that Grear is dead."

Grear looked at him, slowly making his gold eyes fade into brown. The dark brown hair darkened to a midnight black. "Grear's dead." Without another word, he turned and left the room.

He dared to make one stop in the home he used to share with them. He didn't take anything remarkable. Standing by the portrait they'd had painted on their wedding day, his hand stroked Bella's image. The artist had captured the shade of red of her hair perfectly. Fin would have it, as well. But only if he could find her in time.

Determination took hold. Tugging the gold band off his finger, he placed it behind a loose stone in the hearth. Maybe one day he could return and reclaim it. Or their daughter would. Artemis was right. Grear had to disappear, be thought dead.

His pack was ready. It never wasn't. Bella had kept it that way. His job, his passion, kept him always on the move. It was his skills that let them know the raid was coming. His talents that would make it so some of the Amari would remain free. Now, though, time wasn't on his side. Fin was on the move, and he had to find her before anyone else did.

Grabbing the rucksack, he hauled it onto one shoulder. A final touch to the wedding portrait. "I'll find where you sent her, Bella. And keep her free. I promise," he whispered.

Without a look back, Grear strode from the home. He didn't bother to shut the door. The raiders wouldn't honor a locked door. He took off for a small alley between a set of houses. Down to the left, where few would know to look, was his exit. One he knew he could keep secret from those who would be looking for other ways out of the city. He lifted the trap door and tossed his pack down the dark hole before sliding in himself. His feet hit the floor while his hands still grasped the handle underneath the door. He let it drop, not caring about the noise it made. Channeling some magic, he watched stone seal around the opening. Should anyone find it now, all they'd see when they lifted it would be solid stone.

The darkness in the tunnel was absolute. Grear knew the way better than most, didn't need the light. The blackness swallowing his heart matched his surroundings. It took seconds for his vision to adjust enough to make out his pack. Crouching down, he slid it into place on his back while focusing on the path ahead. Lorien was a good week's travel by foot, more if he had to go above ground. Fin would be there ahead of him. Alone, scared. Concern for her spurred his feet forward and he picked up the pace. Not making his way to her wasn't an option.

Chapter Two

The orange glow ahead was dim, yet still bright enough to stab at his eyes. He stopped, crouching against a wall. After a week in darkness, even the feeble light ahead of him made his eyes hurt. He knew the process well, knew not to run toward the light until his vision began to adjust to it. His heart, though, wanted nothing more than to run like mad.

That light meant Lorien was above him. The thieves' guild maintained a torch at the intersection of the sewers and this tunnel. The door could only be opened from this side, making it impossible for anyone not coming from Uamh an Amari to gain access to the tunnel. The small opening, located right behind the torch, made it clear to travelers that the end was near. But did Fin make the journey? She was so young, so unaware of the world outside of the caves they'd called home. Was she able to take Bella's instructions to heart, hide herself as she'd been taught?

Would she be there waiting for him to find her? And would she accept the lie he had to tell her?

He leaned against the wall, his stomach in knots. Everything they planned, her safety, depended on his ability to lie. And the Amari were known to tell the truth. He'd never been anyone's pet, had an owner's chain around him, so the possibility was there. But it would cost him dearly. No physical scars, no. But he would age faster than she would. The lie, and repetition of it until she believed it as truth, would cost him his life eventually. His one hope was the debt to the Mother wouldn't come due until she was safe at last.

Steeling his resolve, he rose. They'd discussed this in length, him and Bella. Privately and with Artemis. The price they'd pay was worth it to keep her alive. And hope with the Amari who were now chained and being scattered across the world.

Slinging his pack over one shoulder, he moved the last few feet toward the entrance. The door outlined in the dim light. Pressing his head to the wooden slab, he listened for a clue of anyone using the hallway. The crackling of the torch was the only thing he could hear. He shifted to the left of the door, his right hand resting on the latch. He knew it wouldn't make a sound, but still held his breath. Twisting the knob, the mechanism vibrated in his hand. A thin line of light pierced the narrow gap between the door and tunnel wall. He peered out to make sure the way was empty before darting out as the door shut silently behind him. Like it or not, Uamh an Amari was forever behind him. With luck, Fin was ahead of him.

He found the sewers first. The smell, foul and acrid, announced the way before he made the last turn. He kept to the wooden passages the Guild had built to make passage faster and safer. Not to mention, it was hard to sneak up on a mark if you reeked of waste and vomit.

He stopped the first person he found who moved without a purpose. "I'm looking for someone."

The woman, her blouse tied loosely, leaned against the wall. "Maybe you found them. What you pay depends on what all you want." She looked him up and down as one hand began to pull at the laces.

"Not that kind of someone. A child. Just three or so. Would've shown up a week or so ago."

The woman snorted, "That's a bit young, ain't it?"

"Too young for your line of work, certainly. I'm here to take her someplace better."

Her face softened. "Good. If she stays here much longer, there's no telling who will have her working for them. Sweet thing, but won't talk to no one." She pointed down one of the tunnels. "Go that way. She's made herself a nest between here and the ladder up to Grendal's place."

He took a single coin from his pocket and reached out to give it to the woman. "For your help. And silence."

She took it, her blue eyes widening at the gold being given. "You're really going to take her from here, right? You're not going to hurt her, are you?"

"Yes. She'll be out of here before dawn. And out of the city as soon as I can get us transport with a caravan."

"I've heard stories, you know. About how the Amari got raided and how one princess escaped. You wouldn't know anything about that, would you?" Her voice was barely above a whisper.

"If it's not true, and others come looking, you know nothing. If it's true, and Amari come, then they can leave a message in her nest. I will check it when I can." He walked down the passage she indicated.

The tunnel was darker than the other one. It–only had one exit, up to Grendal's inn. Anyone coming this way wouldn't be exploring. He heard a creaking ahead, followed by liquid cascading and splashing into the muck flowing underneath the walkway. A fresh wave of stench wafted past him as a loud bang echoed through the tunnels. The ladder was close. So should Fin's nest be.

He reached the dead end. A steel ladder, slime dripping from the rungs, reached up to a small door. Huddling in the deep shadows behind the ladder was a small figure. Curled up with her arms hugging her knees, Fin's hair was matted with offal and shreds of produce. Fluid dripped off her elbows.

"Hey," he called out to her as he moved closer. He wanted her to know he was there.

She raised her head. Green eyes, flecked with gold, stared back at him. Fear and confusion mixed with dirt and mud on her face. "Who are you?" she whispered.

He moved closer, kneeling not far from her. "My name's Emile," he said, keeping his voice light. "What's your name?"

She sniffed, wiping her nose with the back of a small hand. "Fin."

"Well, Fin. Today's my lucky day. I've been looking for you."

She scooted back, panic on her face. The gold in her eyes disappeared. "I'm just a girl. I'm no one special."

"I know, Fin. Your mama sent me. She asked me to take care of you until she and your papa can join you."

"You know mama?" she whispered.

He nodded, "Yes. Her name's Bella. And her hair is as red as yours when it's clean." Smiling, he reached out a hand. "Will you come with me, Fin? I'll keep you safe. I promise."

Hesitantly, she stretched forth a tiny hand and placed it in his. His heart leapt as his hand closed around hers and pulled her closer to him. She hadn't recognized him, but did trust him to keep her safe. It was a crucial first step.

He removed the cloak from his own shoulders and wrapped it around her. It would warm her as much as hide her. Glancing up, he checked the distance to the inn above them. It wasn't far, but the trick would be getting her to make the climb. She was scared and cold. Probably hungry. Grendal would help them. He knew that. But the timing had to be perfect for the staff not to see them arrive.

"Stay right here. I'm going to leave a message for your mama and papa. Just in case they come looking for you." He kept his voice even. Bella was dead. Grear may as well be. He was Emile now to her, and had a host of aliases he was known by. But Fin didn't need to know any of that right now. Maybe ever. She needed the hope that her parents were still out there, somewhere.

He fished a piece of chalk out of his pack. Reaching up, he drew a series of symbols on the dry wall. "What that?" she asked.

Glancing down at her curious face, he smiled a little. "It's a code, Fin. I'll teach it to you sometime. But it tells your parents, or any other like you, that you're safe. And we'll come back every ten years to find them or any message they leave for you."

Emile finished writing and put the chalk away. "There's someone up there" —he pointed to the ladder— "who will help us both. He'll give us food, clothes, and let you have a bath. And make sure we can get out of town without trouble. But we have to be quiet first. Can you climb up there with me?"

Fin's head turned up toward the portal in the floor. Her thoughts were plain on her face. Things only came down from there, and they weren't good things. She was scared. Rethinking his approach, he turned his back to her. "Just put your arms around my neck and hold on to me. I'll do the climbing."

Her thin arms encircled his neck. He reached around and helped her wrap her legs around his waist. "All good?" he asked.

"Yes," she whispered. Her voice trembled.

He patted one dirty arm. They'd both need a bath and new clothes, but that wasn't a problem to him. Grendal had been a friend for years now, offering help to any free Amari he could find.

He stood, adjusting for Fin's weight. Grasping the outer pole of the ladder, he eased across the gap between the ledge and the ladder. Falling into the sludge of waste flowing below wouldn't have been pleasant. He made sure his footing was secure before swinging his body over to the ladder fully. Fin's grip tightened a little. "It's fine," he whispered reassuringly. He looked up, mentally counting the rungs between him and the top, and then focused on the one directly in front of him. Taking it one step at a time, he ascended the ladder.

When the inside of the cover was in reach, he stopped. "Don't move," he whispered. He wrapped his left arm around the rung in front of him, making sure he had a secure grip. With his right hand, he reached up and pushed against the metal disk. Faint light filtered through the crack around the cover. Slowly, Emile moved it off to one side. The sound of metal on stone worrying him a little. Pausing before it was fully moved, he listened closely. No footsteps, no talking. The kitchen was empty.

Pushing it off the hole completely, he got far enough above the hole that Fin would be able to climb off of him. "Fin, I need you to move over to the floor. Just take your time. But I can't get out until you do."

Her small body trembled a little, but she did as he instructed. He saw her slide off to one side, her hands grasping the folds of the cloak and drawing it close around her.

Quickly, he climbed out and replaced the cover. The kitchen was closed down for the night. He'd timed it perfectly. The next step would be getting Grendal's attention.

He crouched down, moving toward the wall that separated the kitchen from the bar. Emile fished a small coin out of his pouch. There was a small crack in the wall, perfectly sized for the coin. He pushed it through and went back to Fin. It wouldn't be long now.

She was half-asleep, and frightened. "It's going to be fine," he said. Wrapping the cloak around her even tighter, he put the hood over her head before picking her up in his arms.

"Amain? Is that you?" Grendal's voice was hushed.

Emile turned, facing the man. "Yes. I've got a guest with me." He nodded toward the cloak in his arms. "She's in need of a bath, and some food. We both are."

Grendal stepped forward. "Rumors run rampant, my friend. Are they true? Has Uamh nan Amari fallen?"

Emile nodded, "Stories are for later. She's beyond exhausted. Please. Let me make her comfortable and then we'll talk."

The other man's beard shook as he nodded. "Of course. Staff is gone for the night, except those tending the common room. We'll go up the back stairs. While you both clean up, I'll make some food for you. Then we can talk."

Emile adjusted his grip on Fin, making sure he wouldn't drop her, and followed his friend up the narrow staircase.

Chapter Three

The brandy swirled in the glass resting in his hand. Grendal always kept this room stocked with a small bottle. Grear normally didn't indulge, but tonight he needed something to wipe away the memory of Fin covered in filth.

Stop that, he scolded himself. *Your name's Emile now. That's the one you gave her. That's what will keep her safe.* He didn't look at the glass as he raised it to his lips, his gaze settling on the small form of the sleeping child. Her hair, still damp, barely reaching the blankets tucked around her.

The brandy burned his throat as he swallowed the last of the contents in his glass. She'd been half asleep when he'd gotten her in the bath. Barely aware that he handed her some dried cheese and meat to eat while he cut away the worst of the tangled mass on her head. Too tired to notice the tear that escaped his eyes and traveled down his face.

The hair, once so curly and like Bella's, was now discarded. He knew he was being foolish. It was hair, it would grow back. But the reality of his wife's death, a future of raising his daughter without letting her know who he really was, hit him as he worked the scissors. It cut through him with more precision than the daggers he preferred to fight with.

A low rap on the door interrupted his thoughts. He rose, returning the glass to its spot near the decanter, and worked the bolt open on the door. Easing it open a crack, he saw Grendal holding a tray. He moved aside, opening the door enough to admit his friend. Once Grendal was in, he shut the door behind him.

"It's not much," Grendal spoke as he placed the tray on a small table. "But we had some leftover stew, bread is from yesterday. I heated it up as fast as I could." He nodded, a small grin forming under his beard. "Not fast enough for her, I see."

Emile crossed the room and grabbed one of the steaming wooden bowls. The contents warming his hands as they closed around it. He stirred it with the spoon as he moved back to the chair. "She was exhausted. Barely stayed awake long enough for me to get her clean." As soon as he was settled back into the chair, he scooped up a spoonful of the stew. His stomach clamored to be fed.

Grendal sat in another chair. "It's true, then? Uamh nan Amari is gone?" Sadness tinged his voice.

Emile nodded as he swallowed more of the stew. "About two weeks ago. I don't think many made it out unchained. There's very few of us left that are free."

"What about the rumors? They run wild, my friend. Everything from the royal family being slaughtered to many escaping. Including the cousin to the king and his daughter." His eyes darted between Fin and Emile.

He gritted his teeth, knowing what was coming. "Grear and Bella are dead." A small pain flared across his back as the scar from the lie settled into his body. "Their daughter, though. She is safe. And will remain that way."

Grendal let out an explosive breath. "How? Amain, how are you going to hide her from the world when every Amari and Human alive is going to hunt her down? She's the heir now. All the kings will want to make her a pet. And the Amari will want her to rally the rest to resist."

He put the bowl down, surprised that he'd emptied the contents as fast as he did. "I will keep her safe. I swore an oath. She will know she is Amari, yes. That I cannot keep a secret from her. The rest, however..." His voice trailed off.

"You're not going to tell her any of it, are you?" Grendal spoke just above a whisper.

Emile shook his head. "No, I'm not. I can't. If she doesn't know, she can't speak to the truth of everything if she's ever captured. She can't tell them who she is, who I am, if she doesn't know."

The other man sat back in his chair, confusion on his face. Neither of them spoke for a few minutes, the wood in the fireplace popping to break up the silence. "Why?" Grendal whispered. "Why commit suicide this way?"

Emile looked at the small body curled up under the blankets. Her even breathing, peace on her face. The fear he'd seen earlier when he found her gone. For now. He knew it'd come back soon enough.

"Because this is the only way I could still be in her life, Grendal. It was Bella's idea. She said it would be easier for her to start the rumor with her dying breath if she knew I'd be the one to find Fin. Raise her." He debated getting another glass of brandy.

"Where was she? Ever since I heard the first reports, I've kept my eyes out for survivors. The only Amari that've come through Lorien have been chained. At least, the only ones I've seen."

"Believe it or not, right under your inn. Bella sent her there, told her to stay safe and hidden until someone could find her. She found a small alcove just under the ladder. She was living off of the scraps your staff would throw down."

"I never even thought to look. I'm sorry, my friend. If I'd but known I could've had her safe up here, waiting for you."

Emile shifted his gaze to Grendal. "No. This was what had to happen. She needed to be afraid, experience the feeling of being hunted. She won't forget that. And it'll keep her safer than showing up and having a warm bath and hot food at her disposal. Life will not be easy for us. I'll make it as comfortable as I can, but we can't live rich. We've got to disappear, blend in. Be so ordinary no one will look at us twice."

His friend nodded, "That makes sense. Where will you go now? Can I at least help with transportation somewhere?"

Emile narrowed his eyes in thought. "Are there still trade ships heading to Kaldr? Or has their trading season stopped already?"

"Kaldr? Why would you want to go live with those savages? Half of their land is nothing but ice and snow! The sun doesn't even set all the way in the winter! Even the traders only go to one or two towns."

Emile smiled. "Exactly. It's perfect. We can find a remote village, hide out for a few years. Let Fin grow a bit." His fingers drummed on the arm of the chair. "It's almost perfect, if we can find space on a ship. They're notorious for not welcoming strangers."

Grendal sighed. "I'm not going to talk you out of it, am I?" Resignation settled across his face. "There's still one ship left in the harbor from there. I'll send a runner first thing in the morning, make the inquiry on your behalf."

"No, I'll take her down there myself. You've done enough. We'll take the back way out at first light so no one knows we've been here."

Grendal rose and moved next to Emile's chair. Reaching a hand out, he clasped his shoulder in parting. Emile kept his sight on Fin while he let himself out of the room. He knew he needed to sleep, but he wasn't numb enough yet. Today was the first step. He'd found her. Now he had to get her out of town.

Rising, he slid the bolt on the door again. Too many variables were still at play, too many chances they'd be caught. The Kaldrkin weren't known for keeping Amari as pets. But they were a secretive race. He could be making things even worse.

He grabbed at the decanter and poured himself another drink. Slamming the liquid down his throat, he prayed his choice was the right one. For both of their sakes.

Chapter Four

Reaching into the bowl, Emile scooped up a handful of water and splashed it on his face. Sleep hadn't been easy to come by. Every noise Fin made, each creak of the floorboards on the hallway outside roused him. He had to secure them passage on a ship today. They couldn't risk staying in Lorien another day.

He lifted the covering on the window, peering out to the world. The first light of dawn crept over the buildings, casting as many shadows as it chased away. Good. He needed to get her past the slave market before it opened up. She didn't need to see her friends, people from Uamh nan Amari, being sold as pets. He didn't need to see it, either.

He let the covering fall back into place and crossed over to where she slept. Kneeling, he shook her shoulder gently. "Fin, wake up. We need to leave."

She shifted, her eyes gradually opening. The gold hue staring at him sleepily. "I'm tired," she said, yawning.

"I know. So am I. But you need to hide your eyes and get up. We've got to get out of the city. We're going to get on a ship, go someplace new." He pulled the covers off of her, ignoring her cries of protest.

Pouting, she sat up. Her brow furrowed as she concentrated on making her eyes green. "Why a ship?"

He found the shoes Grendal had left for her the night before. Placing them on her feet, he said, "Because there's too many people here that would make you their pet, Fin. People who would hurt you because you're Amari. Where we're going is a long way from here. It's cold, snows a lot, but the people won't chain you. We can hide easier there." Fervently, he prayed she believed him. And that he was right about the Kaldrkin.

Once the shoes were on her, she eased off the cot. "Is it an adventure? Mama said that I was going on one when she sent me here."

Emile smiled, "Yes, it's part of the adventure. You're going to be on it for a long time, I'm afraid."

Her lower lip trembled. "I don't wanna be on an adventure anymore. I wanna go home." Tears welled up in her eyes.

He pulled her closer so she wouldn't see the same tears in his own eyes. "I know, Fin. But that's not going to happen again. Home is going to be wherever we make it, someplace we feel safe." He broke off the hug. "It's not here, though. But I know where it might be. Grab that nice warm cloak over there"—he pointed to the garment hanging from a series of pegs in the wall— "and put it on. We have to hurry."

She swiped the back of her hand at the tears on her face and did as she was told. Emile straightened and followed her. His own pack and cleaned cloak were next to the one for her. "When we get outside, Fin, you have to keep your eyes green and don't talk to anyone." He slung the pack across his back, then adjusted the cloak over it. "No matter who talks to you or what you see, understand? Once we're on our ship and heading out to sea, you can ask me all the questions you want to."

"What if I get lost?" she asked, her eyes wide with fear.

Smiling down at her, he stretched out his hands. "You won't get lost. I'll carry you."

Reassured, she allowed him to pick her up. He shifted her weight, making sure she was secure, and moved to the wall. Pressing the knot in the wood, a panel slid aside. Together, they moved into the secret passage.

Enough light filtered through the cracks between the slats to make the staircase navigable. Emile paused to reset the door behind them, then started down the narrow steps leading down. "Keep your hood up when we get outside, Fin," he instructed. "It's going to be easier if people don't see your face."

"Why?" she asked, her head resting on his shoulder.

He cringed at the question. There should've been more time before she was faced with life outside Uamh nan Amari. Time before she knew the fear of being someone's pet. "You know how your eyes are gold? It means you can do magic sometimes. And those who can't do it are afraid you'll hurt them. So, they will try to put a chain around you, control you. That's why you have to keep your eyes hidden."

"Do my mama and papa have a chain now?" Her voice, laden with sorrow, broke a little.

Emile stopped at the bottom of the stairs. He looked at her, the tears threatening to spill from her eyes. *Good*, he thought, *she's holding the green color*. Knowing the pain that was going to follow, he swallowed hard before the lie left his lips. "Your mama and papa aren't in chains, Fin. They're dead."

The tears flowed freely as she threw her arms around his neck and buried her head into the curve of his neck. He stroked her hair with his free hand and let her grieve for a minute while he got used to the fresh scar burning into the small of his back.

"Fin, it's going to be okay. I promised you I'd take you someplace safe. But I need you to calm down so we can do that. You have to keep your eyes hidden until we're alone on the boat, okay? It's really important."

She sniffed, "'Cause they'll put a chain on me if I don't?" The fear was back.

"Yes, Fin. They'll put a chain on you. And then you'll have to do everything they tell you."

"I'll be good. I promise," she whispered, her arms still tight around his neck.

Emile reached up and placed the hood of her cloak back over her head. "Here we go," he whispered, and he turned the knob of the door in front of them.

A quick glance told him the narrow alleyway was deserted. Shadows were being chased away by the dawn, though, so he knew they wouldn't have much time. He slid out, shutting the door behind him.

He kept his movement relaxed, unrushed, so as not to draw attention. People tended to remember the person in a hurry over someone who just walked in pace with the crowd. The docks were still a number of blocks away. The early rising merchants were moving about already. Some with empty carts, others trying to get back to their shops with new stocks of fish or packages from the warehouses lining the wharf.

Emile skillfully blended in with the increasing traffic, weaving their way toward the far end of the district. The distinctive figurehead carved on the prow of the ship bobbed with the waves. The creature was something Emile'd never seen before outside of the boats the Kaldrkin sailed. Rumor said they roamed the icy lands, but he'd dismissed them. Now, though, he and Fin might well find out if the stories were true.

He spotted a sailor working one of the ropes securing the vessel to the pier. "Excuse me." He put a hand on the man's shoulder.

The sailor turned, ice blue eyes narrowing in suspicion. "No charity," he responded gruffly.

"We don't seek charity," Emile responded. "We're looking for passage out of the city." He turned his attention to Fin, "I need to put you down now," he whispered.

She nodded and stood next to him after he eased her to the ground. Her arm instantly wrapped around his leg and she leaned in close.

He rummaged in a pocket of his cloak. "Give this to your captain," he said, placing a gold coin in the sailor's hand. "And let him know we wait his reply."

The sailor looked at the coin, then sized the two of them up with a slow gaze. "Wait here," he said and darted up the gangplank.

Emile nodded once, his arm going protectively around Fin's small form. He didn't have a lot of those favors to call in, and he knew it. It would be worth it if the captain agreed to this one, though.

In a matter of moments, another man came hurrying down the ramp. His shaven head contrasted by a bushy brown beard shot with gray. Emile held up a single arm, signaling that they were the ones waiting. The captain responded in kind, darting around others on the busy dock and reaching them.

"How far?" He asked.

"As far as you go. We need to disappear for a while."

The large man glanced down at Fin, then held a hand out to Emile. "Name's Corbin. And I am honored to aid those with need."

Emile grasped it, "The need is there, or the request wouldn't have been made."

"Let's get you both on board and secure. We'll move out as soon as we can." He began to bark orders to his men, telling them they needed to depart for home.

Emile picked Fin back up and walked onto the ship. Time to find out if the Kaldrkin would keep them safe.

Chapter Five

Emile piled the furs on top of the table. "Jamin! I'm back," he called out. He unbuttoned the toggles keeping the coat closed, shaking off the loose snow as he shrugged the garment off. The warmth of the room quickly melted the flakes into a small puddle underneath the rack of pegs jutting from the wall.

"I'll be right out!" Fin's voice called out. The tenor of her voice cracked slightly. She was getting older.

What did you expect, he chided himself. *It's been almost ten years. She couldn't stay a child forever.*

Her slight frame emerged from the door leading to her room. The red hair hanging down her back, swaying as she moved. His heart constricted. Every time he saw her, he saw Bella.

She moved to the table, her hands caressing the top pelt. "These are beautiful, Redal! Moira is going to pay well for them."

He sat on a bench and began to remove his heavy boots. "She'd better. We have to pay our passage back to Lorien somehow."

She swung her head toward him, fear crossing her face. "Lorien? Why?" The words came out as a whisper.

"It's time. I told you our years here wouldn't last forever. We have to go back, check the message in the sewer. And move on." He rose and crossed the small space to where she stood. "I'll keep you safe. No one will know you were even in the city."

Pulling one of the wooden chairs aside, she sank into it. "But I thought we were safe here. The Kaldrkin are friends now. No one even suspects that I'm..." her voice trailed off.

"I know. It's been a haven when we needed it. But we promised to return to where I found you every ten years. In case your family or more Amari came looking for you. So they'd know you were safe."

Panic flew across her face. For a brief moment, the true shade of her eyes flared before she regained her control. "How can I be safe when they trade in my kind there? I heard the stories that Corbin tells down at the tavern. My kind is treated as slaves! They've even started calling a chained Amari a pet! Why can't you go? You can move freely in their world. I can stay here, wait for you." She chewed her bottom lip. Just like she had every other time she was afraid.

"No, you can't stay here. Corbin spoke with me when he returned from his last voyage before the ice came. Inquiries were being made, rumors being spread. They know some Amari survived the massacre. He was questioned about any passengers he took on about eight or nine years ago. It's not safe for us here anymore."

She lowered her head into her hands, the red hair spilling across her arms. "But I don't want to run again. I'm happy here," she whispered.

"It's time to put aside Jamin and Redal and take up Fin and Emile again."

Shoving her chair back, she stood quickly. "I don't even know who that is!" She sprinted for her room, slamming the door behind her.

Emile slouched in his chair. *Bella*, he thought, *you never warned me that she would be this difficult at this age.* He pushed a hand through his hair. She had to go, that wasn't the question. How to convince her to go willingly, though, he had no idea how to accomplish.

A quick rapping at on the front door pulled him out of his thoughts. Rising, he crossed to the door. One hand grasped the blade he always kept tucked into his waistband. A friend most likely, but Corbin's warning made him cautious.

"Redal! Open up! It's freezing out here!" Thrane's deep voice carried a sense of urgency.

He opened the door, standing aside so Thrane could enter. His daughter, bundled in furs to ward against the cold, followed him into the home. Both headed to the fireplace to get warm as Emile shut the door.

"Where's Jamin?" Thrane asked as he pulled off his thick leather and fur gloves to warm his hands.

"She's in her room. Thrane, what's wrong?"

The other man nodded once to his daughter, who took off toward Fin's room. "The preachers are coming. Faster than Corbin thought they would. There's a couple in Moira's place even now, stirring up trouble." Thrane moved away from the fire and sat in a chair next to the table. "Redal, they're saying girls can't become warriors. That it's wrong for them to go through the trials. One of them even claimed that we have Amari here and that to allow them to be free was an affront to everything decent in the world." He sighed. "Soon as the elders started to nod like the crap made sense, Bryn and I left and headed here. Someone started asking about a door to door search as we did."

Emile sank into a chair opposite of his friend. "Dear gods," he whispered.

"Look," Thrane said, "I don't give a damn if you and Jamin have secrets. We all do. But you're both decent people. If she's Amari, you have to get out of here. Tonight. By morning, they'll have her chained up as a pet."

Emile couldn't reply, he simply nodded his agreement.

"Corbin's ship is getting ready to head out now. I can get you both on it, if we move fast. With one condition."

"What's that?"

"Take Bryn with you. Let her be the warrior she's meant to be. She's trained, can keep Jamin safer than your daggers will."

"You want me to take Bryn away with us? I can't promise we'll ever be back here, Thrane."

A haunted look passed over Thrane's bearded face. "I know that," he whispered. "But she needs to leave. She's no Amari, but the warrior's life is what she's best at. If the preachers have their way, she'd be married off and told to obey her husband. That's not the life I want for her. She'd wither and die." He lowered his head, his gaze focused on a spot on the table before him. "I know my daughter, Redal. She will not bow to a man. It's not how I raised her, or what her mother would've wanted for her. She'll keep your secrets, make sure Jamin stays free."

"You know, then?" Emile's voice came out as a whisper.

Thrane nodded, meeting Emile's gaze. "I think we're the only ones that do here in town. The only ones certain, anyway. A few others might suspect, though."

The door to Fin's room opened with a bang. She stood there, in her heaviest cloak and a pack slung across her shoulder. The pale face reflected determination tinged with fear. Bryn stood right behind her. The older girl's stance told Emile that Thrane was right. She'd die before she gave up Fin.

"You're ready, then? We need to leave now," Emile told Fin.

She nodded once, slowly. Her hair was hidden beneath the voluminous hood.

Emile rose, and held out a hand to Thrane. "Thank you, my friend. You won't be forgotten."

Thrane stood and grasped it in parting. "Corbin's going to be waiting for you three. I'll stay here, tell them you're out checking traps or such. I may not be able to buy you much time, but hoping it's enough."

He turned to Bryn, "Be well, daughter. You are a warrior. Honor the memory of your mother who taught you how to be both woman and warrior."

Bryn nodded once, her dark braids swaying with the movement. "I will honor you both, father."

Emile darted to the peg by the door and slid his heavy coat back onto his body. The pack lay on the ground where he'd left it when he came in the house. He shoved his feet back into the boots, one at a time, before positioning his hood or grabbing for his gloves. "We'll take the back path, the one that leads behind the smithy. It's dark enough now that we shouldn't be seen. And it gives us more buildings between us and Moira's tavern."

He straightened up and leveled an even gaze at Bryn. "No matter what, you get her on Corbin's ship. Do I make myself clear?"

"I know my duties, Redal. And will fulfill them."

He reached for the pack, slinging it over his shoulder. "Good. By the way, think on a new name. We'll have to change who we are before we get to Lorien." He moved the latch off the door and swung it open.

Outside, the snow was coming down hard. He looked around, making sure no other villagers were nearby, then waived Bryn and Fin to come out. Intently, he watched the snow fall into the prints around his door. They were filling quickly. *Good*, he thought. The storm would both mask the direction they went and keep others indoors.

He followed the other two as they moved as quickly as the terrain allowed, keeping his eyes and ears open. Part of him also kept watch on Bryn, admiring how she made sure to look about before allowing Fin to move forward. Thrane was right. She was going to be as protective of Fin as he was.

They arrived at the docks quickly. Corbin's ship was a dark mass out on the water, illuminated only by the falling snow. For a moment, Emile's heart sank. The ship wasn't tied to the dock but in open water.

Catching up with Bryn and Fin, the older girl pointed to the edge of the pier. A small rowboat sat, waiting. Corbin stood inside, his hand rested on the final pylon, waiting for them.

Emile dashed over to him, "We need passage, tonight."

Corbin smiled at him. "Why do you think I'm waiting here? Come on, all of you. I want to be to sea before the town becomes more like the rest of the world."

Emile made sure Fin and Bryn made it into the boat first, then lowered himself in. "What's the rest of the world like nowadays?"

Corbin dipped the oars in the water, moving them forward with each powerful stroke. "Crazy," was all he said.

They stayed silent as the small boat moved to the ship. Emile kept his gaze on the shore, intent to spot the smallest movement that would indicate pursuit. Fin sat next to him. He glanced her way once, his heart breaking at the silent tears that trickled down her cheeks. She was right. Life in Kaldr hadn't been perfect, but they'd had more good than bad. Fin had made friends, learned how to be a normal person while hiding her true self. Bella would've been proud of her. But he didn't dare tell her that.

The questions about her mother had stopped after a year. The nightmares took longer. When it was late, and she slept at last, he'd let the façade drop and hold her as Grear. As her father. The lie and mask he wore for her was beginning to wear on him. The last hunting trip he was on brought it home. The stake, hidden in the snowbank, skewered his foot. The pain he felt healing himself was even greater. His ties to the earth, where the Amari drew their magic from, was eroding. He'd only have another ten years or so before it would be gone forever. At that point, his life would end.

Face it, Grear, he scolded himself. *You should've taken her back to the mainland two years ago. The only way to know she's safe when you're gone is to find others to do the job you've been doing. Like Bryn. She's going to need more than just you soon enough.*

A soft thud told him they arrived at Corbin's ship. Turning, he saw a rope ladder drop from the side of the vessel. The captain signaled Fin to ascend first. Bryn followed quickly. As Emile waited his turn, two more ropes dropped down. Taking his cue from Corbin, he slid one through a ring at the end of the rowboat, tying the rough rope securely. He then began the climb up the ladder.

Fin stood off to one side. Bryn hovered behind her, holding a warrior's ready stance. The sailors that dared look their way quickly went back to their duties after a single glance from Bryn.

A hand touched his shoulder and he turned. Corbin pointed toward the front of the ship. "Take my cabin," he said, "Get the ladies inside and out of sight while we get under way. We'll talk later."

Nodding his agreement, Emile waved at the other two to follow him. The ship rocked gently beneath him. Corbin's deep voice shouted orders to his crew as the trio wove their way past them and into the cabin.

The room hadn't changed much in the last decade since they'd last been on the ship. Dark wood decorated the room. A bunk built into one side, framed on three sides, rested under a glass window. The panes were frosted with the sea spray. The table was bolted to the floor slightly off center so anyone could enter the room and move around freely.

Emile slid his pack off and placed it in a protected corner. "Packs can go here," he said. He looked at the ceiling and saw hooks far enough apart for a hammock. "I'll ask him where the hammock's stored and sleep in that. You two take the bed."

Fin, her pack tossed carelessly in the corner, climbed up on the bed and sat in a corner closest to the window. She turned her back to him, pulling her knees up under her chin, and stared out the window. Every part of her body screamed at him to leave her alone.

"She'll be fine…eventually," Bryn whispered. "She's not a child anymore. Not yet a woman, and I don't think she'll ever be a warrior, but no longer a child."

Nodding, he kept his voice low and even. "I know." The ship's motion shifted. The anchor was up and they were picking up speed. "I'm glad you came, Bryn. She will need your help for a few years. There are things about being a woman I simply don't understand."

"There are things about being a man a woman cannot understand. This is normal. Oh, and my name is no longer Bryn. She will be hunted for ignoring her 'rightful' place at the hearth and choosing a warrior's path."

He stopped studying Fin's still figure and turned to look at the other woman. "Good. What will you be called?"

"I am Gwen. Who are you now? I do not think Redal and Jamin are on this ship."

"No," he sighed. "We will become Emile and Fin, for now. That may change, depending on the city we are in. Do not be surprised if it does."

She shrugged. "If it keeps her safe"— she nodded to the silent figure on the bed— "then your name matters not. That is our goal, correct?"

Emile looked back at Fin. She'd shifted, resting her head against the wall. She wasn't taking this well, and would blame him for some time for uprooting her life. But he promised Bella to keep her safe. "Yes, it is," he replied.

Chapter Six

Sunlight filtered through the frosted glass, both warming and illuminating the cabin. Emile sat at the table, fingers drumming across the surface. Fin hadn't said a word to him since they'd come on board two days earlier. She would laugh and speak with Gwen, but any conversation from him was met with a stony silence. The tension between them rose as she continued to give him the silent treatment. Gwen forced her to go out on deck just now to separate them.

"Damn it, Bella," he swore under his breath. "I never knew it would be this hard." Frustration made him restless. Fin refused to listen whenever he'd try to bring up what they would do when the ship docked in Lorien. It was as if she planned to stay on Corbin's ship until it went back to Kaldr.

Rising, he crossed the small room and pulled out his pack. He rummaged through it, his hands blindly seeking out the leather notebook he kept at the bottom. Where Fin wouldn't find it. At least, he hoped she wouldn't.

He sat back at the table, grateful for the pen and bottle of ink that were secured to it, and opened the book to the marked spot where he'd left off. Dipping the nib into the ink, he began to write.

"She doesn't know you do this, does she?" Gwen's voice broke through his thoughts.

Startled, he jerked his head toward the door. She'd come in without a sound, and shut the door behind her. "No," he said, as he shut the book. Replacing the pen and capping the ink bottle, he continued, "And I'd rather she never did. Not yet, anyway." He rose, clutching the journal in his hands.

"One day, then? She will know everything?"

He went back to his pack and put the book away. "Yes, one day. When I'm gone and she's ready to hear all of it." Glancing over his shoulder, he watched Gwen as she leaned against the door. Only he couldn't tell if she was listening in case Fin came into the room. Or to keep him from leaving it.

"When do I get to know everything?" Gwen's face was calm, but unrelenting.

Straightening, he leaned against a cabinet. "When I think you need to know, you will be told."

Her gaze locked onto him, "I cannot protect her from harm if I don't know where it will be coming from. I know she is Amari. I know she believes her parents are dead, killed in the great raid a decade ago. That you found her in a sewer, covered in filth. But I do not know who you are. Or why you rescued her."

He met her gaze, thinking about how much to tell her, when the vision hit him.

The great courtyard of Uamh nan Amari, covered in dust and rubbish after years of being abandoned, surrounded them. Gwen stood between a madman and Fin, another warrior at her side. Two others, one an Amari woman with hair almost as red as Fin's, climbing the stairs that encircled the courtyard. The man carried himself with the same regal air Artemis often had. Fin, lying on the ground, her body all but buried beneath chains. A man next to her, trying to uncover her and set her free of the weight. A bow lay discarded next to him.

He saw Gwen be cut down, her blood spilling onto the carved surface beneath her body and swirling about. And knew that his last act would be to slice open the throat of the madman.

He heard a scream as darkness overtook him.

* * * *

His head throbbed. Emile raised one hand, his fingers gently massaging his temple in a vain attempt to relieve the pain. He wasn't ready to open his eyes yet.

"It's dark in here. I didn't light any lanterns, just the one candle. I was concerned it would bother you when you woke up." Gwen's voice broke through the ache.

He opened his eyes and focused on where the sound came from. She sat near the door, watching him.

"Are you Emile again?"

He pushed his hands down, surprised at the give beneath him. Moving his head, he saw the blankets beneath him. She'd moved him from floor where he'd passed out onto the bed.

"Fin?"

"Is dining with the captain. She did not see what I saw."

His eyes narrowed, "What did you see?" he asked as he forced himself to sit up and swing his legs off the edge of the bed.

"I saw a man whose hair and eyes changed color. You are Amari, same as she is." There was no fear or condemnation in her voice.

Nodding, he replied, "Yes."

"And Fin does not know."

"No. And she can't know."

Gwen nodded. "I think we need to have this conversation in the light." Rising, she moved to one corner of the room and used the candle to light the lanterns hanging from the ceiling.

Emile watched her, waiting. She'd seen him fall, lose concentration. She knew what he was.

When she was done, she returned to her chair. "Why can she not know?"

"For her own protection. If she's ever chained, she can't reveal what she doesn't know. It isn't a lie if she's ignorant of facts."

"I cannot protect her if I don't know who, or what, to watch for. To simply say she is Amari and needs to stay free is not enough. No person should be enslaved, regardless of their race. There is more at play here. I need to know it all."

"Her mother died sending her to that spot in the sewer," Try as he might, he couldn't keep the catch out of his throat. He still grieved for her. "I rescued her because it was part of the plan. The one her parents created, along with the royal family, to give hope to those who would be chained by the end of that day."

Gwen's eyes opened wider, "You are her father, aren't you?" Understanding flashed across her face.

He nodded once. "She thinks he died along with her mother. In a way, the man I was did. I ceased being Grear and became Emile. It's in that anonymity that she and I both stay safe."

"Why did you pass out?"

Folding his hands together, he leaned forward with his elbows on his knees. The headache was slowly subsiding. "We all have different talents. Much like a human who can shoot a bow is different than one who can bake a pie without it burning. While we all have the capacity to do magic, the strength and type varies. I can heal myself a little – all Amari can heal – but I have visions of the future sometimes. That's what happened. I haven't had one since the raid."

"And what did you see?"

He raised his head and met her gaze. "Nothing I can share. It was proof that Fin will survive and be free for another ten years, nothing more." His foot burned slightly as the new scar formed from the lie. "There are more that will join us before that happens. At least two more. I need to keep my eyes open so I know them when we cross paths."

She shook her head. "I don't know if I like this keeping of secrets. It would do her good to know her father still lived."

"Look at me, Gwen. Do I look like the man you saw on the floor?"

Her braids swayed as she shook her head.

"Because I am Emile. This is the man she's known for the last ten years. Not Grear. To tell her the truth now, when we're not speaking already…. It will not help her."

"What about the book?"

He glanced over at the packs. Near as he could tell, the pile was undisturbed. "I've written letters to her, as her father, in that book. When we find an Amari I can trust, I'll give it to them for safekeeping. They'll give it to her when I'm gone." He turned back to Gwen. "This illusion I maintain is going to kill me one day. I knew that when I agreed to put on the mask and raise her. But it was the only way I could stay in her life, even if she didn't know who I was." His voice broke slightly. "I would love for nothing more than to be her father again. Be with her mother, raise her together. But the humans took that future from us. Bella died to save Fin. And I will die to keep her safe."

"As will I," she whispered.

Emile nodded. *I know you will*, he thought.

Gwen rose, "I'm going to go get us food, bring her back with me. I told her you were ill. She does care, Emile." She paused, one hand on the door handle. "I told her she was being silly to blame you for taking such good care of her. If a promise was made to go back to Lorien every ten years, then that promise will be kept."

Emile watched her leave the room and let out a deep sigh as the door closed behind her. He knew too much now. He knew he could trust Gwen, and how the two of them would die.

And not enough about the others in his vision to be certain it was them when he saw them. How did Fin end up buried with chains? Would the man he saw uncovering her be there before the iron severed her connection to the earth and killed her?

"Damn it, Bella," he whispered into the empty cabin one more time.

Chapter Seven

The air changed, the salty smell became more pungent. More rancid. They were nearing Lorien. *Well,* Emile thought, *at least they still send all of the sewage and garbage into the harbor.*

The ship rocked gently on the waves, but wasn't moving forward. Corbin had dropped anchor, claiming the harbor was full until the morning. Emile did his best to ignore the rowboat filled with boxes that now made its' way to the small cave on the shore.

Fin came up beside him, her shirt fluttering in the slight breeze. He resisted the urge to tell her to go get a cloak. She wasn't a child any more, as Gwen had pointed out, and needed to start making some of her own decisions. Not all, but some.

"What's that smell?" her nose wrinkled.

"Lorien," he replied. "They still haven't figured out that anything they throw away comes back on the afternoon tide."

"And you want us to go there? Eww!"

Leaning against the rail, he resisted the urge to laugh. "We have to, Fin. When I found you, I—"

"I know, I know," she interrupted. "You made a promise, in writing, that we'd be back every ten years in case more Amari made it out unchained. I'm not dumb, Emile. I remember things you tell me." Sarcasm tainted her words.

"Then why did you ask why we were going? Never ask a question if you know the answer, Fin. Or aren't prepared to hear it."

She shrugged. The fabric of her shirt moving over her chest with the movement. For a brief second, the baggy garment accentuated her figure over hiding it. She was growing up, all right. Her body was starting to change. He'd have to talk with Grendal about getting some new clothes for her. Nothing fancy, stuff she could move in. Run in, if necessary. But loose enough to make people think she was younger than she was.

They stood in silence, watching as the small rowboat began to creep out of the cave. The cargo, whatever it was, no longer rested in the middle.

"Emile? What's wrong with me?" The panic in her voice set off alarm bells in his head. Snapping his head around, he caught her as she started to convulse. Her eyes moved rapidly, the color shifting constantly.

Quickly, he knelt and cradled her in his arms. He pushed her head into his shoulder to hide the eyes. A whimper began to come from her, one of pain and confusion. As the shaking overtook her body, the sound grew until she screamed uncontrollably. His cloak wasn't able to muffle the sound. The crew, concerned, stared at the two of them.

Gwen rushed over, kneeling before them both. "What is it?" she demanded. "What's wrong with her?"

His mind tried to make sense of it as he continued to try and calm her in some way. Slowly, the pieces fell into place. She was coming into her magic, and had to have earth around her. Not water. "Damn it," he swore under his breath. "Not now, not yet. Hold on, Fin," he whispered. Looking up, he said, "She needs to get to shore. Now."

Gwen started to reply, one hand on Fin's shoulder, when Corbin reached them. "What's wrong?" he asked.

Emile met the captain's gaze. "She has to get to shore. Tonight." *Please don't ask why*, he thought.

Grunting, the man nodded once. "Fair enough. We'll get her in the boat as soon as it's back."

"I'll get our packs," Gwen said. She laid one hand on Fin's hair gently, then rose and ran across the deck to their cabin.

Emile kept Fin's face hidden, fervently praying that the seizure would stop before they had to get on the boat. He didn't want to run the risk of the crew seeing her eyes. He sat, gently rocking her form as the screams and spasms racked her body. Gwen came out, packs in hand, and went to the side of the ship. "It's back," she called out to him. "They're securing it to raise now."

Nodding his understanding, he whispered, "Fin, I know it hurts. Every single part of you is on fire right now. I can help you, but we have to get off the ship first. Please, I need your help. You have to control your eyes. Just long enough for us to get to shore. We'll hide there for a few nights, and get you through this. But I can't do that without your help."

She stopped screaming. Her chest heaved as she took a few deep breaths in an attempt to calm down. "What's wrong with me?" The words came out broken, punctuated by more deep breaths.

He raised his head and scanned the deck. The crew was trying hard not to stare at them, but he knew they wondered. "Not here. It's not safe. Soon, though. I promise."

She nodded, one hand clutching at his cloak.

"One step at a time," he told her. "Gwen's putting the bags in the rowboat now. They brought it up to the side of the ship; you won't have to climb down to it. But there's going to be some of the crew in there with us. We won't be alone until we get to shore." He brushed some hair away from her face. She raised her head to meet his. Her face gave away her fear, and the pain still coursing through her body, but her eyes stayed green. He shifted his arms, giving her space to get her knees underneath her, but kept a firm grip on her in case she fell. "Let me get up first," he instructed her, "then I'll help you. I'm not going to leave your side until this is over."

Sniffling, she nodded again. The process was slow, and he saw her grimace several times before she was standing. He draped one arm protectively across her shoulders and moved at her pace.

Gwen stood in the rowboat, her face blank. The warrior in her wouldn't let the crew see her concern. She met Emile's gaze as they both helped guide Fin in and got her seated. Draping a cloak across Fin's shoulders, the other woman took a seat across for her and grasped her hands.

Emile sat next to Fin, one arm around her. Glancing up, he caught Corbin looking at them as the boat began the slow descent to the water. The captain threw a pouch down to him. The jingle of coins reached Emile's ears as he caught it. "Not much, so use those wisely. Something tells me you'll need to call on a few favors that are owed to me." He put one hand out in parting, then retreated back out of sight.

Quickly, Emile hid the pouch in one of his boots. He wasn't about to look at the contents until they were alone. Corbin he trusted. His crew, not so much.

A small cry from Fin refocused his attention. Her head was down, her hair hiding her face from the oarsman. Just to be safe, Emile placed the hood of her gray cloak over her head. Her body still shook, but the tremors were less.

The oars sliced through the water, moving them closer to shore with each stroke. The same cave where Corbin's crew stashed their smuggled cargo waited for them. Emile scanned the rocky shoreline. They'd have to go deeper into the cave to hide for a few days. Until this passed, Fin wouldn't be in any shape to travel. He only hoped the cave went deep enough for them to have a fire and not be spotted.

The oarsman brought them up close to the rocky beach just inside the cave. Emile motioned for Gwen to get out first. "Fin, we're here. Gwen's going to help you while I get out. You'll feel better soon. I promise," he swore to her.

Her head bobbed in understanding and he used his arms to guide her and keep her steady while Gwen pulled her onto the shore. Stepping out, he watched the crew begin to head back to the ship.

Scanning the cavern, he saw the path that led deeper into the depths. An unlit torch hung in a rung set into the rock wall. "Gwen," he said, pointing to it, "we'll need light to get further in." He put both hands on Fin's arms and studied her face in the meager light still coming into the cave. It was pale, but the shaking had subsided at last. Her muscles still twitched from pain, but she was handling it. "Once Gwen gets the torch lit," he told her, "we'll go as far back into the cave as we can get. Stay warm and dry, have some hot food. And get you through this."

"What's happening, Emile? You promised you'd tell me..." her voice trailed off, pleading.

"When an Amari turns a certain age, the true strength of their magic comes to them. You've always had the capability, and could do small things. But you need to spend time to adjust to what you're truly capable of. And find out what you're best suited for. It may take a few days, but we'll wait."

Her eyes widened, "But, the anniversary. We don't have the time to wait long." It was the first time she'd ever told him she knew the exact date.

What else do you remember and haven't told me? he thought. "There's time," he reassured her.

Orange light filled the cavern with a glow as the torch sparked to life. Gwen stood, holding it out to Emile. "You lead. You know where we're going. I'll make sure we're not followed."

He glanced at Fin, and she nodded. "I can walk now," she said. Her voice shook slightly, but was stronger.

Moving to Gwen, he took the torch and started to make his way down the tunnel.

The room was well hidden, in a side cavern with a large boulder blocking most of the entrance. Someone used it regularly, given the cots and blankets that sat ready. A raised fire pit sat in the center of the room. A small table with chairs sat against one of the walls.

"Won't we be found? I mean, it's ready for someone to come here." Gwen asked.

"No one will, not for a while yet. It's safe." Emile reassured her. "Corbin's used this cove for as long as he's been sailing. This is a good place for him to hold meetings with people he doesn't want to be seen meeting." He watched as Fin lowered herself onto one of the cots. "You can go ahead and light the fire. I'm betting there's something we can use for food over here." He moved over to a small chest. Lifting the lid, he found a well-stocked pantry. A couple of pots, some bowls, and enough dried beef and vegetables to make a decent stew.

"Is it edible, though?" Doubt tinged Gwen's voice.

"Yes," he replied as he pulled out what they would need. "He's got a deal with a local farmer. They come in every few days and restock the vegetables. And keep the entrance hidden. In return, Corbin makes sure they have enough gold to keep their house in good repair." He moved over to the table. Pulling free his dagger, he started to cut up the foodstuffs he'd removed from the chest.

"Is that where we'll go next?" Fin asked, her voice trailing off.

Emile looked her way. She was stretched out on one of the cots, her eyes heavy. He stopped chopping and laid the knife down before crossing to her. Pulling a blanket across her body, he said, "Eventually, yes. But just to make it easier for us to get into Lorien. Rest, Fin. You need your sleep right now."

She sighed, her eyes already closed. "Mkay," she muttered before falling asleep.

Weariness threatened to take over his own body. He sat heavily on one of the other cots.

"What is wrong with her, Emile? Not what you will tell her when she wakes. But the truth."

"Nothing's actually wrong, Gwen. I didn't see the signs that she was coming into her full potential is all. Had I seen it, we would've been off the boat before it hit." He looked at her, "Amari get their magic from the earth below them. When the time came, she was on water. Surrounded by it. That's why she reacted like she did. Had she been here, it wouldn't have been as severe."

The woman nodded in understanding. "What comes next, then?"

"She rests, probably for some time. And then I teach her some very basic things. Nothing that someone who wasn't Amari wouldn't know. It will give her enough knowledge to know what to do if she ever has to call on that power. And I'll teach her about the scars. It's not much different than how she hides her eye color. She's been doing that for a long time now. This won't take her long to master."

He rose, moving back to the vegetables. "Until then, we eat. Keep a watch while she sleeps."

"I thought you said this place was safe?"

"She's Amari, unchained, and on the verge of coming into her full power. She's a long way from being safe."

Chapter Eight

Emile watched her, trying to find any sign Fin hadn't recovered fully from the onset of her magic. She'd slept all night and well into the next day. He and Gwen had taken turns on watch. Even though he told her the cave was a safe place, he wasn't entirely ready to relax. Not until he knew what Fin was now capable of, and if she could control it.

"You can stop watching me, Emile," Fin's voice carried across the small chamber. "I'm not going to collapse again.

"I'll be the judge of that. I've seen more people go through what you just did than you have."

Her head snapped around, her gold eyes glaring at him. "Well, maybe if you'd let me be what I am, this would've been easier to deal with!" She spat the words out.

He leaned forward, resting the palms of his hands on the table, and rose to meet her angry stare. "If I let you be what you are, Serafina nan Grear, you'd have a chain around you somewhere and be someone's pet!"

Frustration boiled in him. Ever since they'd left Kaldr, she'd been rebelling against him. Testing his resolve to keep the secret, and his authority to decide what was best at every turn. *Maybe it's time to start showing her what life for an Amari really is like*, he thought. Straightening up, he found his pack and tossed it onto the table. Pulling at a string securing a side pocket, he said, "You want to have an idea of what it's like for your kind in this world?" he asked. His fingers burned briefly when he found what he was looking for. Tossing the iron bracelet at Fin, he challenged her, "You think your life is hard? Try putting that around your wrist and then pick the lock. I dare you!"

She reached for the object as it flew toward her, like he knew she would. A painful scream ripped out of her throat when she caught it, instantly dropping it onto her cot and staring at her hands.

He crossed the room, holding out a hand to Gwen to tell her to stay put. This was between him and Fin. Either the girl got it in her head that staying hidden and scared of everyone was in her best interest, or they might as well walk into Lorien and surrender.

Standing above her, he pointed to the bracelet. "That's iron. It's not a pure metal. Any time an Amari has something that's been altered by a forge, it does more than burn. It severs your connection to the earth, corrupts it. It forces you to obey the person who put the band on you. You become their *pet*. Begging for food or water, doing whatever they tell you to do. Pick it up," he commanded.

She finally looked up at him. Tears streamed out of her eyes. She'd changed the color back to green. Fear and pain still plain on her face. "I…it hurt…" she stammered.

Part of him wanted to stop right there. But things like this was why he was chosen to raise her. Even though he longed to be her father, embrace her, tell her everything was going to be fine, he couldn't. The only way she'd live a life without one of those bracelets on her was to drive the point home.

"Pick it up," he commanded, tossing a set of lock picks onto the blanket next to the bracelet. "Try and pick the lock."

Swallowing hard, she reached for the items. Her hands shook. As soon as she touched the bracelet, she jerked her fingers back.

"That's why I won't let you be who you really are, Fin. Because I made an oath to your mother and father never to let one of those bracelets touch you. We had it easy in Kaldr. They didn't care. The rest of the world is going to fear you, want to enslave you. Only because of what you are, what you can do."

She looked back at him, whispering, "But what am I? A monster?"

"No. You are Amari. You can do things the rest of us can't. Except do harm, even by lying. If you do, your power will rebound. The pain you cause others will scar your body, cut into your very soul, depending on what you do. The ones out there," he gestured toward the entrance to the room, "won't care. They're going to force you to kill others and not care if it kills you in return." He softened his tone. "And it's my job to make sure they never get the chance to use you as a weapon."

She bowed her head again, rubbing her hands against her trousers. He knew they were stinging. It'd taken him months to be able to pick up anything iron and not wince. But they didn't have the time for her to ease into it.

"Is that my real name?" she whispered. "I barely remember hearing it."

"Yes. Your mother gave you that name."

"Is she dead, Emile? Or wearing one of those," she pointed at the shackle in front of her.

"She's dead. She used every ounce of magic she had to send you to the sewers under Lorien where I found you."

He willed himself to stay still and just stand there, not reach out for her. "An army was descending on your home. Humans who were intent on enslaving every single Amari they could find. She sent you away so that you'd never know what it felt like to have one of those," he pointed at the pile of metal on the blanket, "touch your skin."

Her shoulders slumped as the weight of his words, of Bella's sacrifice, sunk in. "What else, Emile?" Her voice was subdued, scared.

"What else what?"

She looked up at him, "What else do you know? About them?"

Sighing, he pulled a chair over to the cot and sat in it. His arms draped over the back as he studied her. "Your mother's name was Bella. She had the same color hair you do. She had a talent for healing, and taught school in Uamh nan Amari. Your father's name was Grear. He had a cousin that worked for the king," he paused as pain flared briefly on his back. "They had a small house near the central courtyard of the city. And they loved you very much."

"How did you meet them?"

"I used to do some minor trading, mainly of information. I met your father when he was on a hunting party one winter. Meat had gotten scarce, and I needed a place to ride out the winter. I helped them hunt without being found by local humans, they gave me shelter. Bella was pregnant with you when we first met."

"You're not Amari, then?" The wistful tone in her voice broke his heart.

"No, I'm not." Pain flared again, longer and deeper than before. It was all he could do to resist rubbing his side.

"How do you know so much about them, then?"

"Your mother trained me. I told you, she was a teacher. She taught me everything I would need to know to help you when your magic woke up, about how iron and steel would burn when you touched them. How the magic the Amari have comes from the earth itself, and how the humans would force you to misuse it to the point of death." Unable to resist any more, he reached out for her hand. "She taught me these things to keep you safe. You're only thirteen, Fin. You need to be afraid in order to stay alive. Gwen and I," he looked to the young woman that studied them both, "we're here to keep you safe. But we can't if you fight us. There may be more folk, as we travel, that I'll want to add to the group. That's up to me to decide. I need

199 • Amari: Three Tales of Love and Triumph

you to stop fighting me on things, though. What we do, where we go, is based on where I think you'll be the safest."

"I understand now." She paused. "Will you ever tell me everything, Emile?"

He thought of the book, buried deep in his pack, and what it said. "One day, yes. You'll know everything. But not yet."

"Why not?"

He sat back, his hands grasping the back of the chair. "For your own safety. If you're ever chained, Fin, you won't be able to lie. Ever. If you do it now, you'll get a scar from the magic rebounding on you. It's considered doing harm. If you don't know the entire story, you can't reveal it even chained. It keeps you, Gwen, and me all safer."

"That's strange."

"What is?"

She sighed, "You say it makes us all safer. But it only makes me feel more alone."

"Welcome to the human world," Gwen said.

Fin's shoulders slumped. Emile couldn't tell if she finally understood or simply gave up fighting. It didn't really matter, though. As long as she let them guide her, keep her safe. *It's far better that she's afraid now*, he thought, *than anything else.*

"So, what's next?" she asked. "If my parents are dead, why risk going into a city like Lorien? There's not going to be any message in the sewers from them."

Emile's heart constricted at the defeated tone in her voice. He felt Gwen's eyes on him. Looking over, she shook her head slightly, warning him. She was right. Coming clean to Fin right now, even though he wanted to do it more than anything, wasn't going to help he'd just told her that Grear was dead. He had to live the lie he uttered.

"Well," he said, rising from the chair, "we go into Lorien. The codes I inscribed into the walls weren't just for your parents, Fin." He moved the chair back to the table as he spoke. "It's a code, developed centuries ago. Back when the Amari first started to be enslaved. If any others made it out of Uamh nan Amari, they'll leave their mark. And let us know if there's a safe haven that's been found."

Fin raised her head, her face half hidden by her red hair. He could see strength mixed in with the fear on her features. "Is there ever such a place for an Amari?"

"We can look. Keep you free, come back to Lorien every ten years. And hope."

"Hope for what?"

"That we'll find more free Amari. Or at least someplace where you're safe, even for a few years. I'd like to move us around, keep us from being too settled for a while. Your abilities have woken up. We may not be able to stay in one place for more than a year or two now. Depending on what you're capable of, humans will become suspicious."

"That's half the problem. Fear." Gwen interjected.

Emile nodded. "She's right. The humans fear the Amari, because they're different. They control an energy humans can't. That fear drives their need to control your kind, Fin. They seek to put limits on things they cannot comprehend."

The girl raised a hand and pushed it through her hair. "But they don't even know what I can do. I don't know what I can do. Why would they fear me?"

"Because they don't know. Whatever they don't know, don't understand, they strive to control and limit. It's in their nature."

"You two aren't trying to do that," she challenged.

"No, because Gwen and I know better." Emile chuckled. "I've seen what the Amari can do, and how they live. Their customs and their reverence to the earth.

They're not a race to be feared. Yet the humans do just that." He paused. "As to your other question, you'll know what you can do before we will, most likely. Given your reaction, I'm thinking you're fairly strong. It's just a matter of finding what kind of magic answers your call."

"Can't I just try something and see if it happens?"

"You could, yes. But I don't recommend experimentation. Each time you do something, it comes back on you. If you set out to heal someone, for example, you'll feel more rested yourself. Harm someone, and--"

"And I'll have a scar. The more scars I have, the more likely I'll be found out. Keep to being helpful if at all possible. Got it."

"I hope so, Fin," he told her. "For all our sakes."

Chapter Nine

The last rays of daylight danced across the stone wall. Still under construction, it partially surrounded the city nestled in the valley. It would be dark before they made it, but he didn't want to sleep another night on the road. After three years of constant travel, Emile was ready to put roots down. Even if it was just for the winter.

He glanced back at Fin and Gwen, both leaning against the huge rocks that surrounded the path. "I can see the city. We were told right. The walls aren't complete yet. We should be able to get in easily. I'll get a job on the work crew. That should make it so we can spend a winter here."

Fin nodded and straightened a little. She'd grown, and was now close to being able to look him eye to eye. She'd adopted Gwen's habit of braiding her hair and keeping it mostly out of sight under her cloak. The shadows didn't hide how tired she was, though, and he knew it.

He turned and started to ease his way down the path. The light was fading quickly, and he didn't want to trip. They didn't need another break.

Two years ago, they were coming down from a mountain pass to the east. He couldn't even remember where or what kingdom they were in. But he'd fallen, broken his ankle. And they found out what Fin could do.

He remembered the pain as she knelt next to his feet. Her face taking in the strange angle his foot was in, telling him to hush when he tried to command her to leave him there. Then Gwen was holding his shoulders still and placing a roll of leather between his teeth.

Before he could react, Fin placed both of her hands around his boot. And twisted his foot back into place.

The pain came first, and he bit down hard on the leather. Then he felt the energy, Fin's magic, flowing through the earth and into his body. He rode the wave of calm as it fused the bone back together as if it'd never been shattered.

She was a healer. And a strong one.

"Watch your step," he cautioned as he worked around a small pile of rocks.

"That's your job," Fin countered.

Emile smiled at hearing the slight teasing in her voice.

"This is Caerlynn?" Gwen asked.

"Yeah," he replied. "King there was part of the raid on Uamh nan Amari, but has mellowed since then. A lot, according to rumors I've heard. There's hope that his son doesn't hold the same fear of the Amari that most humans do. It's possible that he'll do the thing his father doesn't have the courage to do when he takes the throne."

"What's that?" Fin asked, slowly picking her way through the bigger rocks.

"To set the Amari in his lands free."

The sound of skidding behind him made him turn. Fin was still upright, one hand on a large boulder. Shock and a little bit of hope showed on her face. "Do you really think so?" she breathed.

Emile shrugged. "I don't know, Fin. The current King won't, but I've heard that his son is more sympathetic toward the Amari. His father may live for decades yet. We'll learn what we can, from any Amari in town that I can safely speak with, while we're there. But the town is still segregated. We won't be permitted to stay in their quarter."

She nodded and started to move again. "Still, it's nice to think that maybe one day it could happen. How old is this King?"

"Not that old," he responded as he moved to a flatter part of the path. The worst of the descent was behind them. They'll still be walking in the dark, but it wouldn't be steep. "Maybe my age."

"That's ancient," Fin teased.

"Be nice," he shot back. "His son's not too much older than you. Maybe I'll have to arrange a marriage while I'm here."

"No, you won't." Gwen's voice boomed loudly.

"Come on, Gwen. Don't you want to wear a crown one day?" He laughed and ducked as a rock flew past his head.

About an hour later, they approached one of the unfinished portions of the wall. Two guards, trying to stay warm at a small fire, stood up.

"No need to get up," Emile called out. "We're looking for an inn for tonight, possibly work tomorrow morning. Any suggestions?"

One soldier eased back into his chair while the other walked toward them. "Go two streets down. Place called Hunter's Horn. The innkeeper should be able to get you set for tonight, tell you who to see tomorrow." He paused, looking the three of them up and down. "What kind of work would you and these two ladies be looking for?"

The soldier's gaze lingered too long on Fin for Emile's comfort. "My sister and her friend would be good in a kitchen or helping around the inn. I can help with the wall."

"Bet the red-haired wench could help out all right," the seated soldier snickered.

Emile stared at the man, waiting for him to become uneasy from the scrutiny. It didn't take long before he bowed his head and returned to his dinner.

"Thank you for your recommendation, friend," he placed a single coin in the soldier's hand. Nodding to Fin and Gwen, he led their way into the city.

The inn was where the soldier described. While not entirely clean, it was well lit. And cheap.

When they got upstairs, Gwen nodded to him and pointed to the door. Curious, he followed her out.

"Go downstairs, Emile. Drink some ale, find work, and don't come back up for a few hours."

Confused, he looked at her, "Why?"

"Did you not see the looks the soldiers gave Fin? She's grown, Emile. She's not a child any more. And certain things may become a liability soon over a virtue."

"I don't understand, Gwen."

She gave an exasperated sigh. "Emile, I'm going to give her an object lesson on what goes on when two people get married. Or at least really like each other."

His eyes widened at her suggestion. "Excuse me?"

"Look, she's grown to where no amount of baggy clothing or cloaks will hide her figure. And I'd rather her first time be with someone who won't hurt her for their own pleasure. We're vagabonds, tramps. Not nobles. Those soldiers wouldn't think twice about taking her in a back alley." She leaned against the door, "You know I'm right, Emile. And it's not like you can do this. I'm the best choice —the only choice—so go have some ale and try to forget what's happening up here." She twisted the knob and walked back into the room, shutting the door behind her.

He stood in the hallway, stunned. Suddenly self-conscious of his own presence in the hall, he turned and went back down to the common area.

A duo were up on a makeshift stage—a man on a drum while his female partner gyrated to the beat. Surveying the crowd, he saw the faces of the men as they sat, mesmerized, by the dancer. Hunger and lust followed her every move. Gwen was right. Fin needed to learn this lesson and he couldn't teach it.

Looking around, he sought out an empty table. Most of the patrons had pulled their chairs closer to the stage. All but one.

He was a large man, taller than Emile. A fighter, judging from his build. The hilt of a sword peeking over one shoulder solidified Emile's opinion of the man.

His eyesight blurred for a moment, and the warrior in the corner became one with his vision from the boat. This was one of the companions Fin would need.

He walked up to the bar and ordered two ales. Grasping a mug in each hand, he made his way over to the corner.

The warrior watched him as he approached. Emile wasn't trying to be sneaky about it. In some ways, he was impressed that the man took his gaze off the dancer. "You looked thirsty," he said, placing one stein on the table in front of the man before lowering himself into a chair opposite of him.

"You look like a man who needs help." The man's voice was deep, but soft. It wouldn't carry farther than Emile. *Good*, he thought, *he knows how to be discreet.*

"You might say that." Emile took a swallow of the ale. "How long are you staying in Caerlynn?"

"Until the wall's built. Or I choose to do something else. You?"

"Same."

"What about those ladies you came in with?"

"We've been on the road for a few years. Figure they've earned a few comforts. At least for the winter."

"And after that?"

Emile leaned back. "Don't know yet, but we'll move on. I don't really like to stay put for long."

"Of course you don't. You're running, all three of you." The man took a drink.

Narrowing his eyes, he looked at the other man, "What's your name?"

He shrugged, "Doesn't matter. I'll be changing it before we leave anyhow."

Emile's body jerked slightly, startled at his words. "Not sure I know what you're talking about, my friend."

He put the mug back on the table, "Let's stop playing games. I know who you are, who both of the women are. I've been waiting to catch up with you for three years. Ever since I saw your last message in the sewers." He chuckled. "You took a few detours I didn't anticipate. Never figured I'd get here before you did."

Emile's stare got even more intense, "Who are you?" he whispered.

"Let's just say that Artemis sends his best and leave it at that." He leaned back in his chair.

Artemis. That was a name he hadn't heard for over a decade, one he hadn't dared utter. He thought his cousin, his King, would be long dead.

A plate of food appeared in front of him. Stomach growling, Emile started to eat.

"Here. You'll not rest until you know everything and this is not the place for long explanations." He slid a sealed letter across the table to Emile.

Shifting seats so his back was to a wall, he broke the seal and read it quickly.

G,

This man was one who came after us in Uamh nan Amari, but did not like what he saw. He begged me permission to pay for his actions that day. So I have sent him to try and find you. I have no doubt you're both still alive. You're too stubborn not to be.

Trust him. He will not fail you.

A

"Trystian." The other man whispered.

Emile raised his head, "Pardon?"

"I think that will be my new name. Trystian. Eat. Enjoy the dancing. We'll go upstairs later and meet the ladies." He tore the parchment from Emile's hand and lowered a corner to the lit candle in the center of the table.

As it caught fire, he continued, "I will swear whatever oath you deem necessary. Tomorrow, all of you will move into the small house I've been able to rent. You and I will work on the wall. They will try to have a normal life for the winter."

Emile gazed at the burning paper, mesmerized. When it was ash, he looked back at the man next to him. "And in the spring?" Emile asked.

He turned his head, the dark eyes showing Emile the depth of commitment this man had for the task in front of him. "In the spring, we keep her safe. And keep looking."

Chapter Ten

The heat of summer met the bucket of liquid as it hit the sand. Steam rose, sizzling in the blazing sun, and the last drops evaporated before they hit the ground. The acrid aroma blended with the other smells of a camp with too many people.

They'd left Caerlynn on time, headed east. Only they weren't in a position to start crossing the desert. Not yet. And certainly not without a guide. So they sat, slowly baking, in the meager oasis town.

Emile stopped, mopping the sweat off his brow with the sleeve of his tunic. He was the only one of them to still wear full gear. He claimed he was afraid he'd burn. When he really wanted to hide the multitude of scars that crisscrossed his body.

"Emile," Trystian called out from the tent flap. "Over there." The larger man pointed off to the distance.

Turning his head, he shielded his eyes from the glaring sun. A caravan was making its' way into the oasis. "Here, take this," he handed the bucket out toward Trystian. "Tell them to stay inside."

Trystian came out far enough to grab it from his hands. "I know the drill. So do they. We stay inside until we know it's safe."

Emile nodded and turned away. They'd not been at the camp long, really, but it was past time to go. Too many slavers with Amari, looking for more pretty women or strong men regardless of their race.

He wove a path around the other tents, avoiding piles of waste and trash. Trystian found a tent for them before they left Caerlynn. It wasn't big, but it kept most of the bugs out.

The caravan leader was shouting orders, commanding his staff to water the horses first. He took care of his animals. Good. It mattered to Emile.

Studying the group as he got closer, he saw pack mules and shackles but no obvious signs of slaves. He was searching for more. Not good.

He stayed off to the side as the man, clad in white robes, spoke with the relative head of the oasis. The job title didn't matter. He was simply the one that held it that month, and collected rent. He was dark-skinned, weathered. He'd done this for a while.

"Speak, friend. Do not stand on ceremony with me. Or do you think I did not see you in the meager shade of this place?" His voice was soft, friendly.

"You tended to your horse. This is a wise man at work. I would not interrupt," Emile replied.

"Wise men do not like to walk across a desert," he replied, easing the bridle off the head of his steed. Half turning, he nodded. "He is good for now. I take it you have business with me?"

"Maybe. May I ask your name and where you're heading?"

"Rahjin of Antioch. Heading toward Lorien, of all places. Get out when the sun hasn't found the desert, come back when winter has returned. That's the best way to cross." He paused, "And you?"

"Carroll. Looking for a guide for me and my friends."

Rahjin's eyes narrowed, "But not to Lorien. Or Antioch."

Emile shook his head. "No. We're escorting a woman. She's to be wed to a minor chieftain up in some village in the mountains. Guide we had ran off one night. Was hoping you were heading the same way."

The other man shook his head. "No, and you'll need one. It's brutal to cross this time of year. Even skirting it to get to the high lakes where you're aiming to go. How many in your group?"

"There's four of us total. Me, the bride, her attendant, and someone to make sure no one bothers her at night."

Nodding, Rahjin responded, "Her father is a wise man. Shane!" he shouted toward the rest of his caravan.

Looking over, Emile saw another man pause, his head swivel toward them. The late day's sun glinted off the bracelet around his wrist. Placing the saddlebags in his hand on the ground, he moved to join them. His gold eyes framed by long, dirty blonde hair.

"Shane's an Amari. He's traded with me up there, knows the way. He'll guide you to the clan you're looking for. Or get you close enough you'll find others." He paused when the other man got closer. "I'm done with you. This man and his friends need you more than I do. Tomorrow, you free up three horses, yours, a mule, and some supplies. Take them up to the mountains. They have business with one of the clans."

Shane nodded, expressionless, and walked back over to his pack. Emile narrowed his eyes as the man left. He wasn't more than a year younger than he was, and there was a familiarity to his movements.

"It's done. He's gotten his last command from me. Now, he'll obey you."

Taking mental note to both warn Fin and free Shane when they were done, Emile nodded. "What do I owe you, friend?"

Rahjin watched the other man retreat. "Fifty gold would cover the horses and tack. I'll make sure Shane adds a spare tent into the mix. Some of you will have to ride together." He paused, "As to him," he pointed to the retreating figured, "I don't need coin. But, if you're inclined, I'd like you to set him free when you're done with him. He's a good lad. Been with me since the raid on that damnable cave the Amari called home. Too many back home want to buy him, misuse him. I'd like him to have a taste of what it means to be free, if possible. I can't do it. I'd lose all credibility with my contacts if I did." His voice trailed off.

"You're a good man, Rahjin. It will be as you suggest." Emile bowed slightly. Fishing some coin from the pouch at his waist, he handed it to the trader. "We're camped over there," he pointed to their small tent. "We'll be ready to leave at first light."

"Done. I'll tell him to find you when he has the horses ready. That bride shouldn't show up with worn shoes, you know. Bad luck and all."

Emile left, his mind searching for the memory he couldn't locate. He knew Shane, but couldn't quite place him.

Halfway back to the tent, it hit him. For a brief moment, he allowed himself to smile, inwardly rejoicing at the connection. They were in good hands and he knew it. He'd just have to wait for the right time to reintroduce himself. Sometime when Fin wouldn't overhear the reunion.

He moved aside the flap of the tent and stepped into the relative darkness within. Fin rose, followed quickly by Trystian and Gwen. Expectation reigned on her face.

"We have a guide. And horses. We'll be able to leave at first light." He paused. "The leader gave over rights to an Amari in his caravan. The man's name is Shane. Soon as we're in a safe location near the high lakes, someplace we can spend the winter, I'm setting him free."

The anger that flashed across Fin's face dissipated as he finished speaking. "Do you think he'll know who I am? Or you?" she asked.

Shaking his head, he replied, "I don't think so. You've grown since the raid. Even if he figures out who I am, I don't see it being a problem. He's going to be set free for the first time in over a decade. He'll be motivated to stay that way. Which means he'll keep any secrets of ours he might learn."

"What's the cover story?" Gwen asked.

"Fin's a bride, being married off to a clansman up in the Lakes. Gwen, you're her attendant. I'm the noble hired to get her there safely. Trystian's the muscle to make sure it happens. We won't have enough horses for us all to ride, so I'll have Fin with me. We're lighter together than either of you, so it should work."

Trystian grunted, "Plus, you can put a heel to the horse and get her to safety if need be. It works."

Emile nodded. "Right now, I'm Carroll. I didn't give names for the rest of you. Wasn't necessary. Let me know tonight if you want to try an alias until we set Shane free. Until then," he paused, "we eat, pack, and get ready to move first thing in the morning. I want the dust of this place behind us well before noon."

He watched as the rest nodded and started to reach for packs. That wouldn't take long, he knew. Especially since they'd wait for morning to pack the bedrolls. But it distracted them.

And that was a good thing when you were waiting.

* * * *

Dawn's first light was slowly creeping over the horizon when he woke. Trystian stood over him. "It's time. Our guide is here."

Emile rose quickly, "Wake the others," he commanded as he moved to secure his bedding. Once he was done, he shouldered his pack and tucked the roll under his arm. "I'll be outside," he said, "Once everyone's out, we'll drop the tent and get moving."

Exiting the tent, Emile saw four horses and a pack mule waiting with the man he'd seen the day before. He studied Shane, looking for any signs of recognition as he secured his gear. The blonde man kept his focus on the animals and didn't look his way.

"Carroll." Fin's voice broke through his thoughts. Turning, he saw her holding her own gear. She looked past him at the Amari, curiosity on her face.

"Hand it here," he told her. As he secured her packs, he said, "Yes, that's Shane. Stay away from him until we know if he'll keep secrets or not." His voice was low.

She nodded once, her reply as soft as his had been. "Why wouldn't he? Why would Amari turn on each other?"

Tightening a strap, he grunted, "Dunno. But I do know it was another Amari that told the location of Uamh nan Amari to the humans. One that thought he would be granted a reward for turning in his own kind. Sorta sours your hope that Amari are above all of that."

It didn't take long for Trystian and Gwen to take care of their gear and the four of them got the tent packed up in short order. Emile lifted Fin onto a horse, then swung himself into the saddle behind her. "Shane, we need to head to the High Lakes. Please, show us the way."

The Amari turned in his saddle and looked at Emile. For a brief second, he thought he saw a glimmer of recognition on the man's face. The stony resignation came back. "As you command," the man intoned. He put heels to his horse and began to head out of the oasis, leading the pack mule with one hand.

Emile looked at Gwen and Trystian and waited while the woman took the next position in the line. The warrior would follow on his horse. Mounted or on foot, they knew how to defend Fin.

The dark outline of the mountains wavered in the early morning light. They were days away yet, but at least they were moving again.

Chapter Eleven

The first night in the mountains relaxed him more than he thought it would. After the bleakness of the desert, it was a comfort having trees around him. The temperature began to cool within an hour of their climb off the wasteland surrounding the base of the mountains.

"We should find a place to camp soon," Shane called out.

"Why? It's barely past noon." Emile responded.

The Amari shifted in his saddle, "With respect, this terrain changes quickly. And it grows cold at night. Your bodies are used to the heat. They will not respond well tonight if we push further into the forest. There is a lake nearby. It's fed by the mountain itself, and is warmer than most. A good place to bathe if the ladies are in need of such comforts. The first settlement is still a good two days' ride, no matter if we stop or not."

Emile nodded. "Sound reasoning. Find us a good spot, Shane. We could all use a bath and a hot meal tonight."

Within the next few hours, they'd found a spot. True to his word, the hot springs were nearby.

Trystian surveyed the surrounding area. "Surprised no one's here already," he muttered.

Emile squinted at the tree line surrounding the small clearing. "The locals are reclusive. Tend not to come down this low. Like Shane said, we're still a few days from the closest settlement. Outside of traders, I don't see us being disturbed." He tossed the tent canvas to the ground. "Let's get these up, though. And it won't hurt to keep watch tonight."

"I don't need nobody watching me bathe."

"Understood. We let Gwen watch over Fin, I'll take Shane down. I need some time to chat with him anyway."

The big man's eyes narrowed, "You suspect something." It wasn't a question.

"Suspect, no. It's more of I know who he once was. At least, I believe I do. He may know who I was, too. I'd rather get that cleared out before something slips where Fin can hear it."

"That's why I'm here," Trystian replied, tossing a pole into the pile. "Make sure she doesn't hear things she shouldn't."

"Is that the only reason?"

"No, but it's the only one I'm sharing tonight."

Emile accepted that answer. It wasn't often Trystian talked about what he did back in Uamh nan Amari. What his role was during the raid. Only that he had to make amends somehow.

"One day, my friend, you'll have to tell me your reasoning."

Trystian grinned, "Not today, though."

Once the camp was set up, Emile sent Gwen and Fin down to the springs. Shane kept to himself, tending to the horses and refusing the chance to sit near the fire when dinner was ready. He took a bowl, bowed slightly, and went back to the animals.

When Trystian came back, he knew it was time to get things straight with their guide. Causally, he walked to where he sat against a tree.

"Trystian's back. Grab some clean clothes. It's our turn."

The man looked up at him, caution reflected in his gold eyes. "It is not often a master would bathe with his pet."

"I'm not into men, if that's what you're afraid of. I had a wife once." His voice trailed off. "Besides, if they're all clean," he gestured back toward the camp, "the ladies won't stop complaining about us."

Resignation crossed the other man's face. Emile had an idea of what he thought might happen. There were plenty of stories, and things he'd seen, about what happened to Amari when they got into the wrong hands. Things that made him shudder. However, there wasn't anything he could say here to reassure Shane. What needed to be said had to be done away from camp.

They walked in silence, Shane leading the way. When they came to the hot springs, Emile made a show of leaning against a rock opposite the other man and taking off his own boots. He wanted to make sure to time things perfectly.

"How much have you guessed?" he asked.

Sputtering, Shane swiveled as he placed his shirt on a rock. "Nothing. I know nothing."

"Really," Emile replied, keeping his voice calm. He pulled his shirt off. The skin of his chest and abdomen criss-crossed with scars. The sight made Shane's eyes widen. "You've gotten better at hiding your thoughts, Titus." For the first time in years, he allowed his disguise to dissipate entirely.

"Grear?" Titus gasped, his voice barely above a whisper. "If you're here, then…" his face turned back in the direction of the camp.

He put the illusion back into place. "Yeah. It's her. I'm going to be freeing you, by the way." He tossed the small cake of soap over to his old friend. "We've got a lot to talk about, you and I. Most of which she can't overhear. But we still have to come back clean." He laughed. "You start."

Titus waded into the water. "Not much to tell. I got caught trying to lead a group out of the caves. None of us got away. It was horrid, a nightmare. The humans were evaluating us like livestock. Anyone they felt was too old was slaughtered without pause. Too much Amari blood was shed needlessly those first few days.

"We were chained immediately. Even the youngest. Grear, I pray you never hear an infant wail in pain like that. I still have nightmares from that night."

"How'd you end up in Rahjin's caravan?" Emile asked, dunking his head quickly.

"Pure luck. He was in Lorien when we marched into town. Bought almost fifty of us at the auction, I think. He's a good man. Tried to keep families together when he could. Others, like that Island King, were more interested in separating us. Rahjin treated us well during that first march across the desert. His home, though, has some of the same outlook for the Amari as Lorien and the rest. We're nothing but pets, slaves to do their bidding. What they had some of our kin doing…" he took a deep breath. "Grear, be glad Bella died. She was spared a far more painful life."

"Why the name change? You couldn't lie to them once they chained you."

"They made us change our names. Started calling us something new simply to try and break us. Make us forget what it was like to live free." He passed the soap over to Emile. "Your turn. Obviously, you found her. I'd heard rumors."

He looked at him, "Really? The rumors have started then?"

Titus nodded, "All of the Amari in Rahjin's caravan have heard them. How a single princess, with red hair, escaped. That she'll one day lead them to freedom. It gives them hope. Too bad she kept her hair covered when we left the oasis. It would've added fuel to the fire."

"What name is attached to this 'princess' of theirs?"

"Serafina. Lyssa comes up every now and then, but it's almost universally accepted that she died in the raid and that Serafina was saved to carry on the line." He paused again, "How much does she know?"

"Almost nothing. And I mean to keep it that way." Emile found a submerged rock near the edge of the pool that he could sit on. "The only thing keeping her and I both out of chains and alive is her ignorance. If she ever is banded, she can't tell them what she doesn't know."

"Damn," Titus whispered in shock. "That's gotta be killing you."

"In more ways than one. I need your help, Titus. Stay with us for a while. She needs an Amari to teach her to control her magic. I can't without revealing who I am. To her, I cannot be Grear. I must remain Emile. She knows you're Amari, and is curious as anything. Don't talk about culture, etc. If she asks, tell her you never lived in Uamh nan Amari or were taken too young to remember. She has to stay ignorant of that. But she still needs to control what she's capable of."

"What's her talent?"

His mind went back to the night on the mountain. "She's a healer, believe it or not. And a strong one. She managed to put my ankle back together without hesitating. Stay with us—teach her. We're going to be up here for a few more years. I'll take us through Antioch, hire a guide, go over to Dunegan for a while. Eventually make it back to Lorien again in time for the anniversary." Emile paused. "When you leave us, I'm going to give you something. Head over toward Caerlynn. The king there is decent, but his son's going to be even better. Even if you don't stay, make sure the package does. With an Amari you trust. I'm sure we're going to end up back there again when our group's full."

"More visions?"

He nodded, "Yes. There's one more, someone that's going to protect Fin in ways a father can't. And Christoph's going to be the King his father can't afford to be. One day,

Caerlynn will become the haven we've sought for the last fifteen years." He paused. Something wasn't right. "Get dressed. We're not alone."

Quickly, they both climbed out of the pool and rubbed coarse towels across their bodies. The unease he felt grew with each second. Soon as his foot was back in the second boot, Emile started to run up the path leading back to their camp. Titus was right behind him.

Strange voices reached his ears as the camp's fire illuminated the clearing. Waving Titus to stop, he hid behind a large tree trunk.

"I said, drop the swords!" A strange voice commanded. "I'll slit her throat if you don't!"

Emile peered around the tree, searching for the speaker. A large man, dressed in furs, held Fin around the waist. The dull silver of a blade glinted in the firelight as it rested against her throat. Gwen and Trystian stood, swords drawn, opposite them. He could make out the faint outline of bows with notched arrows, but the archers were hidden by the tents.

Carefully, Gwen and Trystian lowered their weapons to the ground. He felt someone tap his arm. Titus looked at him, motioning that he was going to circle around to the other side. Emile knew what he planned to do. Walk into the camp, distract them, and give Emile the opening he needed to free Fin.

Clenching his jaw, he nodded once and watched his friend disappear into the darkness. He then turned his attention back to the camp and waited.

"That's better. Don't know who told you to come here, but we don't take kindly to strangers. Especially the filthy Amari," the man holding Fin growled.

Emile eased his way around the tree, keeping his body low. He pulled a blade out from its' sheath at the small of his back as he made his way behind the closest tent.

Trystian kept his hands spread wide. "We don't mean any trouble. We got lost down in the desert. The mountains looked a lot more comfortable to us. Didn't see any signs saying this land belonged to someone. Now, let my sister go and we'll pack up. Get out of your way."

"Where's the Amari? Give him up and we'll let you go. Until then, she's mine." Emile saw the man's arm flex, tightening his grip on his hostage.

"Master, I found the wood. I hope it's enough," Titus called out as he sauntered into the light. He held a few small sticks and one larger branch. Big enough to swing and do some damage.

Leaping out from behind the tent, Emile sank his dagger into the back of the man holding Fin. She kicked him at the same time, ducking fast enough to avoid the blade near her neck. Gwen and Trystian made for their swords. Titus dropped the kindling and swung the branch as he charged.

"Fin," Emile called out, "are you okay?"

"Yes," she said.

"Get behind Gwen and stay out of the way." He ordered her as he ducked the sword being swung at him.

The other two were making short work of the archers. Emile couldn't see where Titus was. The man he was fighting was fast. More than once he narrowly danced out of the way. His shirt, though, wasn't as lucky.

Pain flared behind his knee as one blow came in too fast for him to avoid. Dropping to his knees, he tried to roll but felt the sword slice open his back. Two screams, one male and one female, echoed in his brain as darkness overtook him.

***

Blinking, he tried to sit up. "Don't," a voice commanded him. Emile turned his head toward the sound. Opening his eyes, he saw Trystian rising from a small chair. A cabin wall behind him. "She'll skin me alive if I let you move until she checks you out. I'll be right back." The large man left Emile alone.

A door opened and then shut. Muffled voices. Whoever built the cabin did their job. Turning to his other side, he examined the wall next to him. The seams between the logs were sealed tight with a black substance. He reached a hand up to feel it when he heard the door open again.

"I see you've decided to wake up," Fin challenged him.

"Do I get to sit up and see you, or are you going to stay by the door and just chastise me?"

He heard her latch the door. "Sit up if you must. I've done about all I can do to heal the *new* scars."

Inwardly, he cringed at the inflection she put on her words. Trying not to grimace, he swung his feet off the bed and sat up.

She stood in the shadows of the far corner, arms crossed. Even in the meager candlelight of the room he could see the hurt and anger on her face. "Who are you?" she demanded.

"My name is Emile. I was sent by your parents--"

"Cut the crap!" she screamed at him. "I'm not a child. You're Amari, aren't you? Aren't you?"

"Yes," he admitted.

"And the rest? How many lies have you told me, Emile? Or is it Carroll? Amain? Redal? I don't even know your real name!" Her voice caught.

"You know me, though. Regardless of the name, I am still the same person. Who has had one mission in life for the last fifteen years. The rest was necessary." No longer caring if he hurt, he rose and walked toward her. Each step becoming more sure. "I did not lie to hurt you, nor do I withhold any truth with that goal. I did it to keep you safe. Remember that fight we had in the cave? When we were leaving Kaldr? Do you remember what I told you?" he asked, keeping his voice low.

Tears threatened to spill from her eyes. "You said you'd tell me everything one day."

"And one day I will. I promise that to you. You know one of the biggest secrets now, and must keep it. Should you ever be chained…"

She took a deep breath, "I know. I can't reveal what I don't know." She paused, "It's just that," she stopped.

He read the frustration and anger in her face. "I know. It's hard to try and figure out who you are when you can't be that person. If your parents could've done anything else to keep you safe, they would've. They would not have wanted you to live a life on the run. But it is infinitely better than one as a pet."

"I've been talking to Shane. Wait, no…Titus. He told us that was his Amari name."

"That's good. He'll be able to teach you things I can't. Your talent is closer to his than mine."

"Gwen told me," she hesitated, "she told me that you see things that will happen. And that you knew Trystian was going to join us. Plus one more. Is that Titus?"

"No, it's not." He eased into a chair. "Titus will leave us before we meet the other one. We're going to stay here a few years, let you learn from him how to control your magic. Test your limits." He looked around the room. "By the way, where is here?" he asked.

Fin's laugh held little mirth. "The bunch that attacked us lived here. One of the archers told us about it, signed over the deed so we'd let him live. Promised to tell the rest of the clans to stay away until we quit the place." Looking down at her feet, she shifted slightly. "Titus took out the one that sliced you open without touching him, fell to the ground screaming. It convinced the archer that he was possessed by 'demons' or something. Gwen got in his face, told him that we'd 'summon the demons' again if he didn't keep his word to us. Scared him so much he crapped his pants."

"And Titus?"

She uncrossed her arms, relaxing a little. *Good*, he thought. Her anger was dissipating.

"I was helping you, trying to figure out how to keep you alive. The wounds were so much more severe, deeper, than the ankle. I couldn't see what I was trying to fix. I went to rip your shirt. He tried to stop me. That's when I saw the scars." She looked at him, "He knew, didn't he?"

"Yes. Titus and I were good friends back in Uamh nan Amari. I knew it was him, but he didn't know who I was until we went to the hot springs to bathe." A thought struck him, "How long was I out?"

"Two days. We loaded you onto one of the horses and got you here with the archer's help. I patched you up, with Titus' guidance, and we've been waiting for you to wake up."

"Well, I'm awake now. And starving. Let's see the rest of this place we're calling home for a few years."

Chapter Twelve

"It's set, Emile. I've got a space in the entourage for Rahjin's daughter when they leave next month. When it's time, I'll strike out away from the caravan and head to Caerlynn." Titus spoke softly.

"Good. Rahjin didn't suspect you, then? By the way, that's a good look for you." Emile replied. And he wasn't trying to be funny.

Titus had started to disguise himself before they left the cabin. He grilled Emile any time he could and not have Fin overhear and finally came up with a new version of himself. Bald, a bushy dark beard, and deep blue eyes made him stand out in a menacing way. The scar he'd gotten from taking out the fur clad attacker that almost killed Emile passed as a sword wound. He would proudly display it as a way to keep the curious at bay.

"One more thing, Titus." Emile reached for his bag and untied the top flap. "Take this with you. Make sure it gets to someone who can give it to Fin when I'm gone. I promised her she'd learn the whole truth one day." He handed his friend the leatherbound journal.

Titus took it, one eyebrow raised. "Is this wise?" he asked.

Emile lingered on the book, "It's more secure with you than it is with me at this point. The rumor is growing, spreading. The last one we need to complete this endeavor is here in Antioch. I just have to find him. By the time that gets to her, the worst of it will be over. I hope."

Titus nodded and started to find a secure, hidden spot in his gear for the book. "I hope to see you again, my friend. Before your lies catch up with you."

Shrugging, Emile replied, "What more can a father hope for but to raise their child? Watch them become an adult, someone that can take on the world if they want to? At least I saw that much of her life. Bella didn't."

Without saying another word, Titus grabbed his gear and left. Emile stood, looking at the closed door, for a few minutes. Things were moving fast now. He felt it with every muscle in his body. His time was running out.

Two hours later, the note appeared under his door. Opening the parchment, his suspicions were confirmed. The archer he'd seen with Rahjin's daughter was an Islander, all right. Suspected of being the illegitimate son of the king and an Amari, but not proven. No one had seen his eyes as any color but brown. And, unless you counted a truly uncanny aim with his bow, no miracles or magic performed.

If it was true, that he was half Amari, then that new son-in-law of Rahjin's was his brother. And someone he'd be desperate to avoid.

It was long past time they left Antioch.

Quickly, he threw the few things that weren't packed into his bag and slung it over his shoulder. Gwen and Fin were next door. Knowing Trystian, he was down in the common room already.

"Gwen," he called as he rapped on the door. "It's time."

The door opened and Fin looked at him. Calm, in control. Ready to run again. "We're ready. Where's Trystian?"

"Downstairs probably. We'll sit with him, I'll find the guide we need to get us to Dunegan. Then we'll move."

The three of them moved down to the common room and found Trystian at a table. "Eat now. Not sure when we'll have a good meal again," he told them. And then his gaze began to survey the room.

He found the man he was looking for quickly enough. Sitting alone, an unstrung bow in a protective sheath across his back. To the casual observer, he looked well into his cups. But Emile knew better. And that the archer had already started to watch them as intently as Emile watched him.

Trumpets blared outside as the bridal party began the ceremonial march down the street. Most of the tavern's patrons rose and started to weave out the door to watch. The timing was perfect.

He worked his way through the crowd and sat on a stool next to the archer. "I hear you're looking for a job."

Chapter 13

Fin screamed, pushing her child into the world with the sound. As she collapsed back onto the bed, she heard the wail of the newborn. "You have a son," the midwife said, her voice calm.

A damp cloth wiped at the beads of sweat on her forehead. Looking up, she caught her husband's face. Calm, loving, and tear-stained. "We have a son," she whispered.

"I heard," Alaric replied, placing a gentle kiss on her forehead.

"Where's the book?" she asked. Alaric had stopped reading over an hour ago, when she'd begun to deliver the baby.

"It's right there," he pointed at the table.

She pushed herself up on her elbows. The midwife was cleaning the child in a basin of water. "Was there anything left to read?"

Alaric rose from her side and reached for the journal. "Just another page or two, I think."

"Finish it, please. I need to know the rest."

He flipped the leather binding open and found where he'd left off. Clearing his throat, he began to read.

Fin,

We haven't been in Antioch long, but that's already too long. I never wanted to bring you through here, only I knew we'd meet up with the last person necessary. I am glad you've never shown any inclination to having the foresight I do. It's a curse, knowing what is to be.

Things are moving quickly now. My body is dying. I have, at most, five more years at your side. I don't regret my choice for even a second. I was able to watch you grow, raise you under a disguise, and keep you safe. That was worth any sacrifice I have made.

I give this book to Titus, with instruction that he find someone who will keep it safe until it can be given to you. Under what circumstances those are, I'll never know.

The man we will meet today, the one we will hire as a guide across the desert, will have secrets of his own. Ones that will compel him to protect you like Gwen, Trystian, and I have. Even more so, if the vision holds. I know not if you will love him. But he will love you as deeply as your mother and I did. And I am at peace with that.

I'll leave you with this. Be at peace with what your mother and I did, the sacrifices we made. There was never a moment where we did not love you. Never a time I didn't wish she'd been able to be at our side. And I will die knowing that the woman I raised is beautiful inside and out.

Be well, my daughter.

Grear nan Avery

"That's it," Alaric said as he closed the book.

Fin watched him as he placed the journal back on the table. She finally had all the answers Emile had promised her years ago. While she'd cried several times as Alaric read the journal, she'd laughed as well. Even explained her side of some of the more interesting passages.

"Are you ready to meet your son?" The midwife stood near the side of the bed. The newborn was cradled in her arms, swaddled in blankets.

Fin pushed herself up. Alaric reached behind her, moving the pillows and supporting her with one of his own arms. The midwife lowered the infant into her arms, and she took her first look at his face.

Dark hair, like his father's, peeked out from the top of the blanket. The baby yawned, then opened his eyes and stared at her face. His gold eyes melted her heart. She finally understood why her parents did what they did.

"Do you have a name yet?" Lyssa's voice broke through her thoughts.

Fin blinked, raising her head to look at her friend. Lyssa stood at the foot of the bed, Christoph next to her.

Turning, Fin met Alaric's eyes. He nodded, and she looked back to the infant in her arms.

"He shall be known as Grear nan Emile." Gently, she used one finger to caress his cheek. The infant's gold eyes looked up at her, and she knew her father would be proud.

About the Author

Born in the late 60's, KateMarie has lived most of her life in the Pacific NW. While she's always been creative, she didn't turn towards writing until 2008. She found a love for the craft. With the encouragement of her husband and two daughters, she started submitting her work to publishers. When she's not taking care of her family, KateMarie enjoys attending events for the Society for Creative Anachronism. The SCA has allowed her to combine both a creative nature and love of history. She currently resides with her family and two cats in what she likes to refer to as "Seattle Suburbia".

You can find KateMarie at the following sites:

Twitter: @DaughterHauk

FaceBook: http://www.facebook.com/pages/KateMarie-Collins/217255151699492

Her blog: http://www.katemariecollins.wordpress.com

Other Solstice Publishing Titles
By
KateMarie Collins

Guarding Charon

One should always read the fine print...especially with an inheritance from a relative you didn't know existed.

In a rut doesn't even begin to describe Grace's life at 22. Her ex is using his position as a cop to stalk her, getting her fired from every job she finds. Her parents, not knowing how abusive he could be, believe all her problems would vanish if she'd simply marry him.

After losing yet another job, a lawyer arrives. A relative has died and left her entire estate in Maine to Grace. Eager to shake the dust of Bruce and small town Texas off of her for good, she leaps at the chance. She even changes her name.

Then she learns that her great aunt was a Witch...and the house has some big secrets. Secrets that she has to protect for six months if she hopes to inherit the entire estate and truly be free of her past.

Arine's Sanctuary

The Moreja Sisterhood exists to rescue boys from abuse and arranged marriages. Arine's on assignment, bringing Cavon back to her home in Sanctuary, when she discovers something terrifying.

He can do magic.

When the chance comes up for her to go back out and rescue her own brother, sold off by her mother ten years earlier, Arine eagerly takes the chance. But can she talk him into coming home to Sanctuary with her? And can they get there before the Domine's army, bent on controlling the magic?

Mark of the Successor

Dominated and controlled by an abusive mother, Lily does what she can to enjoy fleeting moments of normality. When a break from school only provides the opportunity for more abuse at home, the sudden appearance of a stranger turns her world even bleaker. Disappearing without a trace, he has left a lingering fear in Lily. His parting words to her mother, "Have her ready to travel tomorrow," is something her mind refuses to accept.

Running away is the only answer. But before Lily can execute her plan, a shimmering portal appears in her room. Along with two strangers who promise to help keep her safe. With time running out, she accepts their offer for escape and accompanies them into a brand new world. A world in which she is the kidnapped daughter of a Queen, and the heir to the throne of Tiadar.

Can she find her own strength to overcome both an abusive past and avoid those who would use her as a means to power?